"*I Was Watching to See How You'd Stand Up Under Pressure.*"

Anger and defiance struggled for the upper hand. "And did I pass your test?" Sandy asked defensively.

"You know you did . . . almost too well."

"Wh-what do you mean by that?"

"You're so much in control of yourself. It's almost as if you've turned off your feelings and operate strictly on logic. I'd guess you're afraid to let yourself relax."

The back of her neck prickled. His words had hit too close to their target. She was aware that she was alone with Carl. She had to get away.

PATTI BECKMAN
and her husband, Charles, have enjoyed playing jazz together since the time they met. Patti has drawn from her own experience and enthusiasm to describe the scenes and characters of her romances.

Dear Reader:

Silhouette has always tried to give you exactly what you want. When you asked for increased realism, deeper characterization and greater length, we brought you Silhouette Special Editions. When you asked for increased sensuality, we brought you Silhouette Desire. Now you ask for books with the length and depth of Special Editions, the sensuality of Desire, but with something else besides, something that no one else offers. Now we bring you SILHOUETTE INTIMATE MOMENTS, true romance novels, longer than the usual, with all the depth that length requires. More sensuous than the usual, with characters whose maturity matches that sensuality. Books with the ingredient no one else has tapped: excitement.

There is an electricity between two people in love that makes everything they do magic, larger than life—and this is what we bring you in SILHOUETTE INTIMATE MOMENTS. Look for them this May, wherever you buy books.

These books are for the woman who wants more than she has ever had before. These books are for you. As always, we look forward to your comments and suggestions. You can write to me at the address below:

Karen Solem
Editor-in-Chief
Silhouette Books
P.O. Box 769
New York, N.Y. 10019

PATTI BECKMAN
Enchanted Surrender

Silhouette Special Edition
Published by Silhouette Books New York

America's Publisher of Contemporary Romance

SILHOUETTE BOOKS, a Simon & Schuster Division of
GULF & WESTERN CORPORATION
1230 Avenue of the Americas, New York, N.Y. 10020

ISBN: 0-671-53585-4

First Silhouette Books printing April, 1983

10 9 8 7 6 5 4 3 2 1

Map by Ray Lundgren

America's Publisher of Contemporary Romance

Printed in the U.S.A.

Chapter One

"What is that man thinking?" Sandy Carver grumbled to her best friend, Julia French. The two women were jostled by a tight knot of sales personnel as they emerged from the latest sales meeting at Van Helmut's department store.

Sandy's large brown eyes flashed angrily. "I know what I'm doing," she fumed. "Haven't I proved myself yet?"

"Of course you have," Julia replied sympathetically. "After the way you've worked yourself up in the department, I'd think Mr. Van Helmut would give you more control. But you know how he is."

"Do I ever!" Sandy agreed. "He's as square, old-fashioned and prudish as a maiden aunt. He knows we sell bikinis in the junior-sportswear department, but he'd rather not think about it."

"He's a stick-in-the mud," Julia chuckled. "But he knows quality. And quality sells this store."

"Sure it does. But there's nothing wrong with a little pizzazz, too. I have some great ideas I know would boost sales. But do you think I'll ever have a chance to try them out with Helmut's Dark Ages attitude?"

The tangle of people unraveled itself, and Sandy and Julia crossed the wide expanse of the carefully arranged furniture department to head for the escalator.

The thick carpet muffled their footsteps. Private conversations burst into laughter as employees enjoyed one last round of early-morning jokes before turning to the serious business of profits and losses, pushing merchandise and keeping customers happy in one of the most exclusive department stores in Houston.

Sandy's hand made contact with the wide, black movable rail of the escalator. Its coolness sent a bitter shiver up her arm.

"Darn!" she exclaimed, as Julia stepped on the moving steps beside her. They began their descent to the first floor. People crowded behind them.

Sandy lowered her voice and leaned closer to Julia. "I just knew he'd listen this time," she said. "A surfing theme is so right for the junior department. We're not that far from the water. The idea wasn't to sell surfing merchandise, just to stimulate the teen-agers to think outdoors, and sun and fun. Now, what's wrong with that?"

"Nothing," Julia agreed, "except Van Helmut's old-fashioned ideas. And since he owns the store . . ." The implication was clear.

"But I'm head of my department!" Sandy exclaimed in a loud whisper. "I know for a fact Carol Langley makes all the display decisions for her department in women's wear. My ideas are just as sound as hers, maybe even better."

"I know, but Carol Langley is mature, forty-five, and has been with the store for twenty years. You're a little too young and pretty for Van Helmut to quite trust your judgment."

Sandy muttered, "Well, whatever the reason, Van Helmut still hasn't given me control of the personnel in my own department. I can't hire or fire."

"Do you want to?" Julia asked, stepping off the escalator.

Sandy stepped to one side, allowing the stream of employees to hurry past her to their assigned departments. Before the doors opened, they had to count out the day's cash for the register and begin to fill out the twice-daily report that they would complete later in the day to verify sales of certain items not on the computer.

"Of course I want to," Sandy said.

"That's not a job I'd like," Julia said, frowning. "I'm glad I'm in advertising, where I don't have to worry about that sort of thing. That's not the kind of responsibility I'd be comfortable with."

"Why not?"

"I'd hate to be responsible for another person losing her job."

"You wouldn't if that other person happened to be Deanna Smith," Sandy said, sighing. "I wouldn't feel the least bit bad about letting her go. She's a real detriment to the department. I think it would be a service to her if she got fired. Maybe she'd straighten up and learn something about the business world. It would do her good to find out she's not as hot a salesperson as she thinks she is."

"Is she still up to the same old stunts?" Julia asked.

"Oh, sure. I've talked to her about not stealing other salesgirls' customers. But she refuses to listen. She hasn't a shred of concern about her for the other people in the department."

"Did you say no one else can stand her?"

"That's right. But it doesn't seem to bother her one bit. All she can think about is her commission and advancement. If she were a hotshot salesgirl, I'd say more power to her. But all she does is encroach on other people's territory, and morale in the department is running pretty low right now. One of my best salesgirls is threatening to quit."

"Does Van Helmut know?" Julia asked.

"Sure. But all he can see is dollar signs. Deanna's sales look so good on paper, he thinks it would be a mistake to get rid of her."

"That's rather surprising," Julia said.

"I know. Van Helmut has a reputation for running a pretty tight ship. He knows the business, and he knows salespeople."

Julia shrugged. "Maybe the old boy is slipping."

"He's not that old," Sandy pointed out. "I'd guess he's around sixty, wouldn't you?"

"No more than that, for sure," Julia agreed.

"He certainly seems robust and healthy enough. I don't think creeping senility is the problem."

"Maybe it's creeping greed," Julia chuckled. She glanced at her watch. "Hey, I have to go. I have a desk stacked up to here." She sliced the edge of her hand across her forehead. "See you at lunch?"

"Right," Sandy agreed.

She watched Julia walk briskly off, admiring her

best friend's tall, lean frame. Julia looked a bit like a china doll with a thin, smooth complexion. Her brown, thick hair was fluffed out around her shoulders. She carried her slight poundage on a trim-boned body and looked smashing in all the latest fashions right off the racks of the junior department. Her small hips and leggy build complemented almost any style she wore.

Had they not been friends, Sandy could have found it within herself to be envious of Julia's appearance. While Sandy was much more stunning than she realized, she had always wanted to be tall. Her five feet, three inches were well proportioned over a shapely figure. She had a well-endowed shape that hinted of a voluptuousness admirers looked at twice. Only those who knew her well realized the coldness underneath.

Sandy had often commented to Julia about how different they were in looks. Where Julia had blue eyes and a thin, elfin face, Sandy had large brown eyes fringed with long, even lashes that needed only a hint of mascara. She had full, soft lips, round cheeks, and a small, slightly turned up nose. Her soft complexion kept her young looking. At thirty, she could easily have passed for a woman in her early twenties.

Sandy's brown eyes darted around her, taking in the familiar scene. Clerks hurried to their departments; money jangled in the registers; coffee cups were thrust under the counters, and the muffled sounds of the opening ritual turned into the sharp clicks of high heels crisply striding across the terrazzo floor.

Just then Sandy saw the newest employee in her

department rush by her. The girl was obviously late. And her outfit was awful! A cheap, ruffled blouse coupled with pants of the wrong color, topped by an ill-fitting, thigh-length vest. Sandy cringed.

"Ellen," she called.

The girl stopped, looked around and smiled nervously at Sandy. It was only her second day on the job, and she had never worked in a department store before.

That was one of the problems with the junior department, Sandy mused to herself. Van Helmut insisted on hiring young girls fresh out of high school. He thought they gave the department a young image. But they consistently caused problems, quit for no reason and had to be coached constantly.

Ellen approached Sandy with a nervous blinking of her eyes.

"Yes?" she said.

Sandy paused. She took hold of her patience and struggled to hang on. "Ellen, perhaps I didn't make myself clear yesterday."

"Is something wrong?" the girl asked, her voice wavering.

"Do you remember what I said about how we must dress?" Sandy asked the question as kindly as she could.

"Oh, yes," Ellen said brightly. She looked at Sandy for a moment. "You mean, this outfit is not right?"

"I'm sorry, Ellen, but it's not. You see, to work at Van Helmut's, you must dress the part. You needn't own many clothes, but the ones you have must live up to the image of the store. We sell quality here, and class. We carry the best in designer clothes."

"But I can't afford clothes like that," Ellen protested. "If I could, I wouldn't need this job."

"I understand that," Sandy said sympathetically. "So I have a suggestion. Why don't you select one nice outfit, something really stylish, and let that be your uniform until you can fill out your wardrobe with other garments?"

"I—I'd like to," Ellen said slowly. "But until I've worked a while, I can't afford to buy anything." She turned her pale-blue eyes toward Sandy. "Am I going to lose my job?" she whispered.

"Of course not," Sandy said. "I'll tell you what, you pick out something you like, and I'll charge it to my account. You can pay me back a little each week. OK?"

Ellen sniffed back tears. "Gee, thanks, Miss Carver," she said, her voice catching in her throat.

"That's all right," Sandy said. "Just be sure you stay on the job long enough to pay me back. I'm trusting you."

"Oh, you won't be disappointed," Ellen said, smiling.

"You see that I'm not," she said, smiling back. "Now, get on with you, and find that outfit. I want you to put it on now."

"Right," Ellen agreed, hurrying off.

Sandy shook her head. It was only March. She'd be very surprised if Ellen lasted until school was out. The girl seemed ambitious enough. She had worked while in high school, but she never stayed on any one job very long. However, each change had been an advancement for her, and perhaps she'd see the potential at Van Helmut's and try to work her way up the way Sandy had done.

Sandy had begun her career at Van Helmut's

department store in the candy department. When she found out it was a lease department and offered no chance for promotion, she began looking for another job. But when a spot in the junior department opened up, Sandy applied for the sales position.

At first, Van Helmut turned her down. Instead of accepting his edict, she marched to his office and asked to see him.

When she walked in, Van Helmut was seated behind a large desk, one of three phones in his hand. A sheer curtain behind him veiled the skyline of Houston in a soft mist of fabric.

Van Helmut waved Sandy to a chair and continued his conversation. She waited, chewing the inside of her lip nervously, but determined to find out why he had denied her request.

It was the first time Sandy had actually seen Van Helmut. She had not been employed long, and so far there had been no general sales meetings, only department gatherings.

Van Helmut was a striking man with a shock of thick, wavy blond hair touched with flecks of silver at the temples. He had large features with an even nose. His jaw was firm, his brows bushy. He wore horn-rimmed glasses and sucked on an expensive-looking meerschaum pipe. The craggy sea sailor carved from the white mineral seemed to offer Van Helmut a comforting companion as he stroked it.

When he hung up the phone, Van Helmut turned penetrating blue eyes on her.

"You insisted on seeing me?" he asked, leaning forward in his swivel chair. He was a large man, an imposing personage, and had Sandy not been steeled for this conversation, his stature and position would have unhinged her.

"Yes, sir," she said evenly, sitting up straighter. She clasped her hands in her lap.

"What about?" He removed the pipe from his teeth.

"About the transfer to the junior department you denied me," she said, meeting his gaze.

"You question my judgment?" he asked.

"No, sir," she replied quickly. "You must know what you're doing. Your department store reflects that."

Van Helmut smiled and leaned back in his chair.

"Go ahead."

Sandy swallowed. She paused momentarily. It wasn't fear that welled up in her; it was apprehension that she might not present her case clearly. Here was her chance to get what she wanted, and she was determined to make the best of it.

"Mr. Van Helmut," she began, searching her memory for the speech she had rehearsed. "I came to see you because you have not had a chance to meet me."

"Oh?"

"Yes, sir. I understand your reluctance to transfer me. I know I'm doing a good job in the candy department. I've checked the figures for last year."

"Have you now?" he asked, his voice taking on a note of interest.

"Yes, sir, I have. And I know there was considerable shrinkage in that department before I was hired."

"Who told you to check those figures?"

"No one. It was my own idea. You see, I didn't

come to work here just to earn a salary. I have certain ambitions. So I've taken an interest in everything that goes on in my department. When you refused to transfer me, at first I didn't understand. Then, as I thought about it, I realized it was probably because I was doing such a good job in the candy department, you didn't want to lose me."

Van Helmut smiled. His blue eyes sparkled with something Sandy interpreted as admiration.

"There's been no shrinkage at the candy counter since I've been there. You haven't lost a dime to theft or to poor bookkeeping."

"That's right," Van Helmut agreed.

"Is that why you refused my transfer?"

"Precisely," he said. "I'm satisfied with you right where you are. Since that's a lease department, you're really under the jurisdiction of the leaseholder, anyway."

"That may be so, but I'm not satisfied to stay there," Sandy said firmly. "It may be good business in the short run to keep me in that position. But in the long run, it would be a mistake."

"How so?" Van Helmut asked, eyeing Sandy closely.

She turned in her chair to face him squarely. "Because I would be an asset to you in another department. The same skills I've used at the candy counter I could use in the junior department. I'm sharp, willing to learn and ambitious. I'm not a fly-by-nighter who's here today and gone tomorrow . . . unless I end up in a dead-end job."

Sandy bit the inside of her lip. Had she overplayed her hand? She didn't mean the last statement as a threat, but she had to be frank with Van Helmut. If he didn't transfer her, she would find a job with opportunities elsewhere.

Van Helmut studied her face, his brows knitted in thought. "How old are you, young lady?"

"Twenty-two," she said. "Why?"

"Twenty-two," he muttered. "Not married?"

"No," she said stiffly, choking back a knot of — bitterness.

"Girls your age are pretty unreliable," he said.

Sandy bristled momentarily at his words. In both age and experiences in life, she was hardly a girl anymore.

"You'll meet some young man, fall hopelessly in love and get married. Then you'll have children, be in and out of the work force, or your husband will find a job in another city, and you'll move and quit without notice. It happens all the time."

Sandy's features hardened. Her vocal cords drew taut. "Not me, Mr. Van Helmut," she said raspily. "I'm not getting married, ever." A tight band squeezed her chest. She fought down an ugly memory leaping in her subconscious. Her mouth went dry.

"Career girl, are you?" he surmised.

"Yes," she said in a hoarse whisper.

His habit of asking terse questions irritated her slightly. She felt as if she were a subject in a research experiment.

"You've got guts, young lady," he said. "That's an asset in this business. I could fire you for your impudence in questioning my decision, you know."

"Yes, sir," she said, her voice meek but her brown eyes defiant.

Van Helmut placed his pipe on a stand next to his desk. He leaned forward in his chair and studied her a minute.

"I'll give you my decision tomorrow," he said.

"Tomorrow?" she asked impatiently.

"Tomorrow."

"Yes, sir," she replied. "And thank you."

"For what?" he asked.

"For seeing me . . . for listening . . . for thinking about it."

Van Helmut smiled. "You've got what it takes, all right," he said. "You're going to do fine, whether here or elsewhere."

"I hope it will be here," Sandy said, rising.

Van Helmut remained mute as she left.

Sandy recalled the incident with a chuckle. She had received her transfer the next day, just as she felt she would.

She sighed. There was no more time for reverie this morning. She was going to have to work out something regarding Deanna Smith. She strode to the back of the store in the direction of her department, waving to several other employees as she went.

Van Helmut's assistant, Jason Hastings, was opening the last door of the store, letting in a light stream of customers.

Sandy arrived at the junior department. Ellen was sorting through a rack of sport skirts. She had a fashionable knit top draped over one arm. Deanna stood at the register, counting the day's register money. Vergie Johnson, the one older lady in the department, who kept an eye on the younger girls, was arranging a new shipment of bathing suits.

Deanna looked up, and her eyes flashed darkly. Immediately she stopped her counting, laid the money aside and marched over to Sandy.

"Miss Carver, Billie sneaked out early last night

and left me to count the money all alone. You know that's against store policy. I had to get Carol Langley from the women's department to recount and verify the amount."

Sandy groaned inside. Why did it have to be Carol, of all people? She was Mrs. Efficiency. A little snafu in the junior department might reinforce Van Helmut's notion that Sandy couldn't manage her department as well as she liked to think. And Carol was the biggest gossip in the store.

Every time Sandy took an evening off lately, something went wrong. She strongly suspected that Deanna Smith was engineering the problems, but she had no proof . . . yet.

"Thank you for telling me about it," Sandy replied mechanically.

She motioned Deanna back to her work.

Vergie looked around, laid down a bright yellow bathing suit and nodded to Sandy.

Sandy strode over to the counter. "Good morning," she said. "I see the suits arrived on time for once."

"Yes, I'm getting them out as fast as possible. The ad came out this morning."

Sandy reached into the large box by the counter and picked up an arm load of swim wear. She examined it closely. She felt the material, checked the seams for width and proper stitching and pulled on the stretch fabric.

"I know," Vergie said. "I'm not sure Mr. Van Helmut would approve. They're not up to our usual quality."

Sandy frowned. "I told the vendor to ship merchandise of equal quality, and he sends us this." Contemptuously, she tossed the suits on the counter.

"If we just had more time before those ads come out in the newspaper," Vergie complained. "You know how the advertising department runs so far ahead. We have to have them a sample sometimes six weeks in advance of the sale. Then, when we can't get the merchandise from the vendor, we have to call the manufacturer and take some kind of substitute. You're good friends with Julia. Can't you get through to her about this particular problem?"

"Vergie, Julia has her own deadlines to contend with. We've discussed this lots of times. It's the kind of situation that has no easy solution. It's maddening, but we just have to live with it."

"So what do we do about the suits?"

Sandy sighed. "Sell them," she said woodenly. "What else can we do?"

"Mr. Van Helmut won't like it."

"He also won't like having an empty counter when the newspaper says we're having a big sale. Sell them, Vergie, sell them."

"And if some of our customers bring them back because they don't hold up?" she asked.

"Give them a refund. We can't in good conscience refuse to take back what we know is inferior merchandise, now can we?"

It was not usual policy to make refunds on bathing suits or undergarments, but when it was a matter of customer satisfaction, Van Helmut's would break almost any rule to maintain its reputation of satisfied customers with quality merchandise at reasonable prices.

Sandy realized her attitude was condescending, but she had bigger worries than a stack of inferior bathing suits. The big spring style show was only three weeks away, and she had to select the best looking outfits from her department for a temperamental model to wear.

Why the girls who modeled for the junior department had to be so difficult, Sandy never understood. Maybe it was adolescent rebellion and lack of experience. They always gave the youngest girls to her, and many of them let their job go to their head. The real pros never caused problems, wore anything selected for them, showed up on time and helped the whole operation run smoothly.

Julia was designing the layouts for the final newspaper ads, and Sandy was supposed to supply a few outfits for the photographer.

"Do I look all right?" came a voice from behind her.

Sandy turned. There stood Ellen in a smartlooking pleated skirt, long-sleeved blouse and bolero.

Sandy eyed her critically. "You look very professional," Sandy commented. "I like it. I think a new hair style would complete the picture. Call the beauty shop and make an appointment."

Ellen frowned.

"I'll charge it to my account. You can pay me back later."

Ellen's eyes brightened, and a smile crossed her lips.

"Now, off with you," Sandy chided. "I want you back on duty in ten minutes."

"Yes, ma'am." Ellen snapped to attention, her face glowing with a smile.

"Miss Carver, there's some new merchandise in the stockroom," Deanna said, as she shut the register. She scribbled a notation on a pad of paper and stuffed it into her little box under the counter.

Deanna took every opportunity to make a sale. She kept an up-to-date filing system of her regular customers and called them when new merchandise came in. Since teen-agers passed through her department so quickly and on into the ladies' department, it was a continuing job to keep track of those who were growing up from the little girls' section of the store and those who were leaving for the women's apparel. But Deanna kept on top of the situation.

Too bad she was such a troublemaker, Sandy thought sourly. She had talked to the girl several times, but since she had no authority to fire her, Deanna sensed the lectures were merely an empty threat. Unless Van Helmut himself chose to let the girl go, Sandy was stuck with her.

She sometimes wondered if Deanna was some kind of a test for her. Van Helmut had usually acceded to her wishes about the department.

She recalled the day she had first confronted him about Deanna.

"She keeps everybody stirred up all the time," she had said. "I think she needs to be put on probation. Then, if she doesn't fall in line, I think she should be let go."

"Talk to her," Van Helmut said. "But I'm not giving you authority to fire her. She's a good worker. She's the type who will make something out of herself. If you handle her right, you can work through the problems she's causing."

"I'm not a counselor," Sandy protested.

"It comes with the job," Van Helmut said coldly.

"Mr. Van Helmut," Sandy said evenly, to keep her voice sounding calm. "I've been with you for eight years. I worked my way up through the ranks. I was the top commission earner in the store for months before my promotion to department manager. I know what I'm doing. Why won't you give me complete control of my department?"

Van Helmut peered at her intently through his horn-rimmed glasses. He didn't speak for a moment. He took a long breath. "Sandy, you're a valuable asset to this store," he said at last. "Everyone knows your reputation as a salesperson. You have great potential, and you've realized a portion of it here."

Everything he said was true, but Sandy sensed a certain reserve in his voice.

"But?" she prompted him.

"Yes, there is a qualification," Van Helmut said. "Sandy, you know I like you personally. Most everybody does. However, you have some rough edges that need to be smoothed out. I know you wouldn't ask anybody in your department to do anything you wouldn't do yourself. That's an admirable quality. But at times there's a hardness about you. It's a trait that stands between you and your high ambitions. You lack a certain compassion. You must realize you're fallible, just like everyone else."

The words stung like deadly arrows shot into her heart.

"I—I know I make mistakes," she said unevenly.

"That's not the real heart of the problem, Sandy," Van Helmut said. "An ambitious person must be tough. You're that, all right. But you also need to be able to put yourself in the other fellow's place. You seem to have trouble doing that. There's an abrupt, distant core to your personality that disturbs me. It seems so contrary to your nature, yet it's there. And it rubs some people the wrong way."

Sandy dropped her gaze to the floor. Her mouth

went dry. If Van Helmut had experienced what she had, he'd be cold and distant, too.

"I don't know what the cause is, Sandy, but you need to work on that side of your personality. You're your own worst enemy. But you don't have to be. For you, the sky could be the limit. You've got what it takes to make it to the top, if you can just bridle that underlying anger that pops out at the wrong times."

Sandy had left Van Helmut's office almost in tears. She had never had anyone talk to her like that before. The wound dug deep. It was true she was reserved, but she didn't think she had to spill out all her emotions just to prove how human she was.

At first, she was so humiliated that she was ready to quit her job. Next, anger crept in, and she decided she'd show Van Helmut just how warm she could be. Then, reason settled on her, and she began a personal assessment.

Maybe Van Helmut had a point. Perhaps she had been so damaged by her past that she had built a steel wall between her and the rest of the world.

She had vowed then and there to examine her reactions to others more closely. It would not be easy to change. Maybe she never would. Perhaps the cocoon was too comfortable for her to break out of. But at least she would try.

It was time to do something with the new merchandise in the stockroom Deanna had called to her attention, she thought, pushing her reverie to the back of her mind. At least when she was alone with racks of clothes, she didn't have to worry about her interpersonal relationships.

The rest of the day passed with its usual hectic pace. The model for the style show arrived for her fitting; Sandy selected seven outfits, from which four would be used in the show, and Vergie was assigned the job of writing the commentary for each choice.

Deanna and Ellen got in a squabble over a customer, and Sandy had to mediate the dispute. Both girls left angry, and Sandy went home with a headache.

The next morning, there was a hot rumor around Van Helmut's that the owner was ill. The rumors persisted until Friday, when Sandy came to work and found little clusters of employees excitedly gossiping about the morning's sales meeting.

Sandy made her way to the employees' lounge, where Julia sat at one of the long tables, sipping a cup of coffee.

"I guess you've heard," she said wryly, glancing up as Sandy took a chair next to her.

"Heard what?" Sandy asked, eyeing the coffee.

"About Van Helmut's son."

"No, tell me," Sandy said eagerly. "But first, let me get something to drink." She dropped her money in the coin box, poured herself a cup of the hot liquid, and glanced around her momentarily. Seated at the table and on the couches along the wall of the white plastered room were excited workers, their faces animated with the latest events. A sense of excitement rippled through the air.

Sandy sat on the straight-backed chair next to Julia. "Well?" she asked expectantly.

"It looks like Van Helmut is going to be out for some time," Julia said. "And his son, Carl Van Helmut, is going to take over the operation of the store."

"Really?" Sandy gasped. "Carl Van Helmut? But I'd heard he and his father haven't spoken in years."

"Be that as it may, it's a very definite rumor that the son is taking charge."

"How accurate do you think the rumor is?" Sandy asked.

"I'd say pretty accurate. It came directly from Van Helmut's secretary."

"That *is* news," Sandy replied, taking a drink of her coffee. It warmed her as it flowed down her throat. She relaxed a bit. "I wonder if he's as inflexible as the old man?"

"Who knows?" Julia chuckled. "But if he's half as good-looking . . ."

He was.

Chapter Two

*C*arl Van Helmut was a young version of his father, Otto. He had the same shock of blond hair, the bushy eyebrows, the penetrating blue eyes. His nose sat in the middle of an unlined face, except for the hint of crow's-feet around the outer edge of his eyes. He was taller, leaner and tanner than his father, but there was no mistaking his lineage.

Carl had the same long, strong fingers of his father, the same imposing appearance, muscular shoulders and commanding demeanor. He could have been a matinee idol, not shockingly handsome, but disturbingly arresting.

There was an expression on his face—as if his eyes could see right through everyone—that was unsettling yet intriguing. He was a man of contrasts. His smile was reserved, his laughter restrained, his anger subdued. He was a man in control of himself and the world around him. He was a man who didn't worry about tomorrow because he knew it would bend to his will.

Sandy and Julia entered the store's small auditorium ahead of a tangle of excitement.

"I hear he's been waiting for the old man to die so he could sell the store," Sandy overheard another employee say. Loud whispers passed back and forth like spitballs tossed in a classroom.

"Naw, he's afraid of his father. He'd never do anything like that," someone else said.

"It's got to be a woman," another voice piped up. "He'd never agree to take over for any other reason. He's got his eye on somebody here."

"You can't tell me that," the first voice retorted. "Carl Van Helmut could have his pick of any woman he wants, but he's still a bachelor. He's never going to get married."

"Who said anything about getting married?" someone chuckled wickedly.

A muffled cackle went up from the bantering group.

"Shhhh, he'll hear you," Julia chided, pointing to the front of the room where the young likeness of Otto Van Helmut stood talking to a group of men.

The gathering broke up into small groups as people took their seats. Julia and Sandy sat in the second row. The small room served both for sales meetings and parties. It was gaily but tastefully decorated with soft yellow wallpaper, brown carpet and brown-and-yellow draperies.

Chairs squeaked and papers rustled as the meeting came to order.

Silence fell over the group as Carl Van Helmut strode to the front of the long table stretching across the end of the room. His sturdy frame reminded

Sandy of a warrior from medieval days. But his clothes were totally modern. He wore dark trousers that slapped around his ankles as he walked, a pale-yellow shirt open at the throat and a plaid jacket.

He cleared his throat. "I'm sure by now you've all heard the rumors, and you can see they are quite true. My father is in bed with phlebitis. I have agreed to take over the operation of the store until he can resume his duties. In spite of what you may have heard, I do know what goes on here, and I am quite capable of handling this position."

Carl's voice exuded confidence. His resonant baritone reverberated through the room and sent a chill down Sandy's spine. It was almost as if the man were issuing a challenge to the group to try to defy him.

Everyone sat quietly.

"The first order of business is the new line," Carl said, glancing at a small slip of paper tucked into his palm. "We want all departments to emphasize gold this year. Jewelry should feature gold, the gold garments in the ready-to-wear departments should be prominently displayed on the mannequins, the furniture with the gold upholstery is to be featured in the traffic areas, et cetera. Think gold, display gold, sell gold. You have until next Tuesday, department heads, to have your new line out, and I want to see the entire store coordinated around this theme. Are there any questions?"

"Yes," said the department head of the linens section. She stood up. "Our gold sheets didn't arrive on time. I've called the vendor, the manufacturer, and put a tracer on the order, but all I get is promises and no merchandise." Exasperation tinged her voice.

"Is this the first time you've had this problem?" Carl asked pointedly.

"No, sir," she replied. "It happens all the time."

"And what do you usually do?" he asked.

"I sell what I have."

"And so you will again," Carl said smoothly.

The woman nodded, smiled and sat down.

"Clever," Sandy whispered to Julia.

"He's foxy, all right," Julia whispered back.

"Now to another matter," Carl continued. "There have been some customer complaints about sales personnel bickering in front of customers." Carl began to pace slowly back and forth in front of the assembled audience. Sandy's eyes trailed up and down his tall, well-built frame. He was strong, she thought, maybe too strong. A shudder ran through her and she forced her attention to his comments.

"When people come into Van Helmut's department store, they are our guests. I think most of you would hold any argument with a family member outside of a guest's hearing. I expect you to do the same here. Customers shop here because we offer quality, we see to their needs and we are always pleasant about it. I want all department heads to monitor their personnel closely for a sense of cooperation on the sales floor."

Sandy raised one eyebrow, glanced briefly at Julia and looked around for Deanna Smith. Now maybe she'd have a little clout with her aggressive salesgirl.

The rest of the meeting was routine, with the usual pep talk and instructions about laxity on the part of the employees. Then they viewed a film on selling techniques.

When the meeting was over, Julia excused herself,

but Sandy remained behind. Carl Van Helmut had given her an opening, and she wasn't about to let the opportunity slip away from her. She waited patiently while Carl discussed several matters with some of the men from other departments.

Soon the room was deserted except for her and Carl Van Helmut. He turned his deep-blue eyes on her. They seemed to reach into her soul and draw something out of her. The feeling disturbed her, and she looked away.

She stood next to the door. For an instant, she wanted to flee. A troubling memory threatened to spill forth into her mind, but she fought it back down and stood her ground.

Carl faced her squarely. He was obviously a very direct man. She turned aside a bit, then straightened her shoulders and met his gaze head on.

"Yes?" he asked, looking down at her.

"Mr. Van Helmut," Sandy began, "I'm Sandy Carver, head of the junior-sportswear department."

"Do you need a word with me?" he asked.

"Yes, I do," she replied. "I didn't want to say anything in the meeting because this is a rather sensitive issue."

"Do you want to sit down?" he offered, indicating a chair.

"No, thank you," she said. There was a more intimate quality about a conversation that took place while seated, she mused. This was strictly business, and she intended to keep it that way.

"There's a problem in my department that I can't handle because my hands are tied," she said. "You mentioned in the meeting about employees arguing in front of customers."

"Yes."

"I can't be sure the complaint was registered against one of my girls, but I do have an employee who has done that on more than one occasion."

"I see. And what have you done about it?"

"I've talked to her, naturally. But I haven't seen any real change in her behavior. That's why I wanted to talk to you. I wanted to find out just how much authority you have in your father's absence."

"Complete authority," Carl said, his blue eyes darkening.

"Then I'm going to ask you to give me hiring and firing power in my department," Sandy said. "This particular girl knows I can't get rid of her, so she refuses to reform. I want to work with her if I can, but I can't get anyplace with her while she knows I can do nothing to replace her."

"Request denied," Carl said bluntly.

"What?" Sandy bristled.

"I said no."

"But why?" Sandy asked belligerently.

"If my father refused to give you that power, I also refuse to give it to you."

"But you said you were in charge now," Sandy retorted.

"That's right, and my decision is the same as my father's."

"Then you might as well be your father," Sandy said tartly. "I thought you might be more approachable. You're younger, less likely to be so rigid. But talking to you is like talking to your father."

Carl's features hardened into granite. He stiffened. The sparkle in his eyes turned into a storm. "Are you always so impudent?" he demanded.

"Only when the occasion calls for it," she shot back.

Carl said nothing for a minute. Then his face softened. He smiled. "You've got your nerve," he chuckled. "But that's what it takes in this business. If you don't get yourself fired first, you ought to go far. You're not scared of the devil himself, are you?"

Sandy stood looking defiantly at Carl for a moment. Then she dropped her gaze to the brown carpet. Afraid. How could anyone know that her bluster was a cover-up for a deep-seated fear she knew she'd never get over?

"I—I guess I stepped out of line," she muttered. It was as close to an apology as she could come.

"You sure did," Carl agreed. "But it shows you care about your department and that compensates for your salty tongue . . . at least in part."

Sandy looked up into Carl's face. There was a soft crinkle around his eyes. His straight, white teeth glistened in a smile.

"You're young," he said. "You'll learn."

"Don't be condescending," she snapped. "I'm thirty. I've been around a long time. I've worked here eight years." How could he compliment her on the one hand and insult her on the other?

An expression she couldn't read crossed his face and settled in his eyes. Sandy couldn't help noticing the smooth, tanned skin, the aroma of a woodsy aftershave that clung to him, the way the room seemed smaller because of his presence. She clenched her fists at her sides. She hadn't even thought about a man as a man since . . . Pain squeezed her heart. She slowly ground her teeth together. She refused to think about it.

"As old as all that?" he said with a wry grin.

Twin spots of pink rose to Sandy's cheeks. She knew he was trying to bait her. It made her angry, but she refused to give him the satisfaction of another verbal battle.

"I have another request," Sandy said, ignoring his comment. "We have some gold bikinis I'd like to display with a surfing theme in my department. Do you have any objections?"

"Not at all," Carl said. "But what did my father tell you?"

"Obviously he disapproved. Otherwise, I wouldn't be asking you," Sandy answered, relieved that she had finally gotten a yes from this man.

"Then my answer is also no," Carl said bluntly.

"But you just told me you didn't have any objections," Sandy sputtered.

"That's right. I don't. But if my father turned down your request, I do, too."

"That doesn't make any sense," Sandy retorted.

"Miss . . . what did you say your name was?" Carl said, obviously exercising his last shred of patience.

"Carver. Sandy Carver."

"Miss Carver, I consider myself merely a figurehead in this store until my father is well. He has given me complete authority to run the entire operation, and until further notice, I will run it just as he would. Nothing will change. Is that understood?"

"Yes, sir," she replied coldly.

"Now, as to your first request, I'll drop by your department and check on your recalcitrant employee myself."

"Yes, sir," Sandy repeated icily.

"Is there anything else?" he demanded.

"No, sir!" she barked like a new recruit in boot camp.

Carl's blue eyes swept over her face one more time, stopping momentarily on her large brown eyes and searching them for something she didn't understand. A nervous jolt shot through her.

She twirled on her heel, squared her shoulders and marched off, heading directly for the ladies' room. She flung open the door, stormed in and immediately vented her anger in a frustrated groan.

She snatched the comb from her purse and nervously pulled it through her shoulder-length blond hair. The thick strands pulled at her scalp. She yanked as hard as she could. The pain felt good.

She slammed the comb down on the counter under the wide mirror and looked at her reflection. Her eyes were narrow with wrath. Her jaw was set hard. She couldn't remember when she had been so furious.

She couldn't go back to work feeling this way. She paced the floor a few minutes, pounding one fist into the other palm, trying to work off the adrenalin pulsing through her veins.

The rest of the day was miserable. Deanna was up to her usual tricks, Ellen came to work late, promised merchandise did not arrive and the table of accessories that had been marked down sat without any buyers.

It was a week later before Sandy saw Carl Van Helmut again. She was helping a young customer make up her mind about a pair of shorts when Carl strode into view. He stood back for a few moments behind a round rack of knit tops, eyeing the scene carefully.

Sandy went on with her business, but Deanna

immediately walked up to Carl and began chatting with him. Vergie frowned as she rang up a sale, and Ellen stiffened, turned a little pale and ran into the dressing room to help a customer.

A few minutes later, Sandy felt a presence come up behind her as she was hanging the unsold shorts back on the rack. She stood immobile. Instinctively, she knew who it was, and she wasn't about to give an inch. If he wanted to speak to her, he'd have to get her attention first.

"Miss Carver?" he said in a low voice.

"Oh, Mr. Van Helmut," she said turning around, mock surprise in her voice.

"I want to talk to you," he replied.

"Here?" She glanced around to see where Deanna was. The girl was hovering around the counter next to the rack with the shorts. She would overhear everything. Perhaps Carl had been keeping an eye on her and wanted to discuss her with Sandy.

"No, over here." He walked off the carpet that delineated the junior department from the aisle and stood near a thick post covered with mirrors on all sides.

Sandy followed him onto the terrazzo floor and stood just out of the traffic area.

"Have you selected your fashions for the upcoming style show?" he asked, eyeing her in a strange way.

"Why, yes," she replied vaguely, wondering why he would be interested. "Everything from this department has been taken care of."

"How are things running in your department?" he asked.

"Except for Deanna Smith, fine." She shrugged.

"I've checked the personnel records, and I find you have an older woman, Vergie Johnson, who has been with the department for some time."

"Yes."

"You also have a new girl, Ellen something-or-other."

"That's right."

"How is she working out?"

"Fine. She's inexperienced, but she's eager and learns fast." Why the inquisition, Sandy wondered. What was he leading up to?

"Then your department could operate without you, if you suddenly were to be absent?" Carl asked.

Sandy stiffened. Was he going to fire her?

"I suppose so," she responded woodenly.

"Good," he said smoothly. "Because I have a temporary assignment for you that will take you out of your department for a couple of weeks."

Sandy took a slow breath. Relief washed over her.

"What kind of temporary assignment?"

"Blanche Donaldson went into the hospital last night. She's had an emergency operation that's going to keep her laid up for a while."

"Blanche?" Sandy gasped. "But she's in charge of the style show. She does all the coordinating."

"Exactly," Carl said. "And she's out of commission. And I've selected her replacement. You."

"Me?" Sandy asked incredulously. Why would he choose her? It was obvious they had a personality clash.

"That's right. I've checked the past records of all the people who might qualify, and you have the best performance of any of them. You're also demanding and serious about your work. You've assisted with several shows in the past, and your file shows you've done an outstanding job on each of them. So the job is yours," he said, as if the matter was all settled.

"Uh, wait just a minute, Mr. Van Helmut," Sandy protested. "I'm not sure I want it. It's true my department is running smoothly right now, but I've still got plenty of headaches. Take Deanna Smith, for instance. I'm not about to leave her under Vergie's supervision. The girl has to be watched constantly, and Vergie doesn't have the authority to control her."

"Is that it?" he asked, studying her closely.

"Is what it?"

"Are you asking for a trade? Power to hire and fire in exchange for taking charge of the fashion show?"

"Well . . ." she stammered. His offer was so sudden that the idea of a barter had not occurred to her. But immediately the sound of it was sweet. "Yes," she said emphatically.

"I like your style," Carl said, smiling. "Under that soft-looking exterior, you're plenty hard. I bet you don't even cry when you get hurt."

Not anymore, Sandy thought bitterly. But she said nothing. Instead, she raised her chin defiantly.

"Okay," he said. "It's a deal."

For a moment, Sandy wasn't sure he meant it. There was a flickering gleam of something in his blue eyes that she read as mirth. Was he pulling a joke on her?

"Is this your decision or your father's?" she asked suspiciously.

"Strictly mine," he said, one eyebrow arching with a meaning that was lost on her.

"I thought you were getting all your orders from

upstairs," she shot back, trying to hide the edge in her voice.

"I said until further notice," he reminded her pointedly.

Sandy stood silent for a moment, considering the offer. "Do I get a bonus?" she asked.

"You don't know when to stop, do you?" Carl accused.

"When the sky's the limit, why not reach for it?" she countered. "I'll go as high as I can. In this case, I don't know what the stakes are, so I'll ask for all I can get."

Carl stood looking at her for a long moment. She was unaware of the people passing by behind her, of the gentle *bleep, bleep* of the computerized cash register in the next department, of the soft flow of air conditioning enveloping her from the overhead duct.

All her attention was riveted on a man who perplexed and disturbed her, a man with deep-blue eyes, thick blond hair and an arresting countenance set in tanned, smooth skin.

"All right," Carl said. Was that admiration she saw glinting in his eyes? "A bonus. But you can just put those grabby fists in your pocket, because you've reached your limit."

"Yes, Mr. Van Helmut," Sandy said demurely, her eyes sparkling with triumph. "Is that all, sir?" she asked, knowing neither of them believed for a minute that she in any way felt subservient to him.

"Why does your 'sir' sound like an insult?" Carl probed.

"The implication is in the ears of the hearer," she rejoined.

"Witty, too," Carl observed.

Sandy hoped he meant that as a compliment, but

the little wellspring of hope spurted for only an instant. It was doused by a bitter, painful memory writhing in the background of her mind, a memory that had shut her off from any interest in men for eight years.

Never again would she allow herself the luxury of losing herself to another human being. The price was too steep. She had paid it once, and she had learned her lesson well. Roland had been an unforgettable teacher.

They stared at each other a moment. Then Sandy looked away.

"See my secretary," Carl said. "She has several items to give you: a list of models hired for the show, the music consultant's name, the name and address of the commentator, that sort of thing. You'll want to get started right away."

"Yes, I'll do that," Sandy agreed. For the first time, she realized how elated she was to be chosen to fill in for Blanche Donaldson. Coordinating the spring fashion show was a tremendous responsibility and a challenge. But she was equal to the task. It was the sort of project she liked to tackle. She was good at her job, and she knew it. She had a sense for style and quality. She had learned rapidly the subtle selling techniques that pushed salesclerks to the top of the commission charts. She had a head for figures, sales reports, inventory control and the many minute details that made up a day in a busy, modern department store.

Sandy took a stack of papers from Carl's secretary and retreated to the employees' lounge to study them. This year's show was to be held at the Holiday Inn in the Royale Room, and arrangements had already been confirmed.

Newspaper ads had started appearing the first of the week, and reservations trickled in. Like past shows, this one would pick up steam with each passing day.

Sandy flipped to a letter of confirmation from Sheila Powers, who wrote agreeing to commentate during the show. Sandy groaned. Sheila had a certain class about her, a well-modulated voice, and she knew fashion. But she rushed the models, often skipping important points of description in her commentary. She tended to take charge of the runway by complaining about the "run of the show"—the order in which the models appeared.

Sandy would either have to find a replacement or make it clear from the beginning that Sheila was under orders from her to run the show according to plan.

Sandy spent the next week working with the modeling agency that would supply the girls to wear the fashions, checking on the building of the 100-foot-long runway to sweep down the center aisle of the tables, handling complaints about clothes that needed alterations and seeing that a lighting crew installed the proper wattage to show off the fashions to advantage.

One morning Carl called her into his office. He was seated behind his large desk. Inwardly, Sandy chuckled wryly. How odd it was to see Carl Van Helmut in his father's chair, acting every bit the powerful department-store magnate. It was like two men superimposed over each other, one older, sterner and proud, the other younger, aloof and intriguing.

Carl indicated a chair. Sandy sat down, clutching a sheaf of papers in her hands.

"How's it going?" Carl asked, leaning back in the swivel chair just like his father. He eyed her critically.

"Just fine," she said confidently. "I'm waiting for a shipment of new styles from the last trip Gladys Haver made."

Carl's face remained immobile.

"She's the buyer in the menswear department."

Carl nodded.

"Julia, in advertising, is begging for something to photograph for our final newspaper display, and I'll have it to her by noon. The runway is almost complete, the models are ready for their final fittings, the music and theme have been finalized and the run-through has been scheduled. We make our final selections for the actual show after we've had a chance to give them another look under the lights in the Royale Room."

Sandy stopped to catch her breath.

"You seem to have everything well in hand," Carl commented.

"I do," Sandy agreed without modesty. "I know the business. And I know how to get things done."

"I'd have to agree," Carl said. He paused. "I'm going to attend the show." He looked at her closely, as if to gauge her reaction.

She frowned. "Oh? Any particular reason?"

"Yes," he said.

Was it to keep an eye on her? Did he not trust her to run things, after all?

"Which is?" she asked.

"I've decided to place a very expensive diamond necklace in the show. I've chosen the clothes I want it worn with and the model. The necklace is much too valuable to trust to anyone. I'll be there to guard it personally."

Anger bubbled up in Sandy. While Carl Van Helmut had every right to do anything he wanted about the show, she felt it was an intrusion on her authority not to have told her about this earlier.

"I have the show planned already," she said bluntly.

"Then change it," Carl said. "You can add one additional model without throwing the entire operation into a tailspin, can't you, Miss Carver?" His accusing tone exploded a bubble of hostility in her.

"Of course I can. That's not the point. You could have told me about this change earlier, that's all." She refused to allow her irritation to rob her of her reason. "I'll handle it."

"I knew you would," Carl said. He rose from his chair and strode around to the front of the desk, signaling that the interview was over.

She stood up. The sheaf of papers tumbled from her lap onto the floor. Carl bent down to pick it up. As he handed it to her, their fingers touched momentarily. His skin was warm. Her hands were icy cold. An involuntary tingle shot through her. She hesitated a moment too long. She looked up into his blue eyes. He was staring down at her, his hand still extended in her direction.

Quickly she pulled the papers to her, protecting her hands between the pages.

"Is something wrong?" Carl asked, obviously aware of her sudden movement.

"No," she said stiffly.

"Sandy," Carl said, his voice deeper and more intimate than she had ever heard it.

The sound of her first name coming from his lips arrested her attention. Her heart stopped momentarily.

"There's something about you," he said. "I don't know what it is. Women usually bore me. But you're different."

"Too different," she mumbled bitterly.

"What do you mean?"

"Nothing. I have to go now."

"Are you sure?" he asked.

"Yes," she said stiffly. Fear began to claw at her. She had to get out of the office immediately. She brushed past him. She knew he was watching her as she hurried to the door. She wanted to look back, but she couldn't. She had made a vow. No men in her life, ever again, not even this one!

Chapter Three

*N*o, she won't do," Sandy whispered to Lydia Adams, head of the bridal department. "She's too tall and not young and fresh-looking anymore. A bride should be small, young and demure. This model is too sophisticated."

Sandy shook her head in disapproval as she eyed the model the agency had sent for the fashion-show finale. It was to be an extravaganza of white and gold with an elaborate wedding dress complete with flowing train and flower girl.

Sandy had made it clear she wanted a certain type of model. Frustration swept over her as she looked at the woman she had been sent.

"You'll be perfect for ladies' sportswear," Sandy said, smiling.

The model nodded and walked on, following a salesgirl to the appropriate department to try on an outfit added at the last minute.

"It's either get another model or pull someone out of the show. Give her fashion to someone else to wear, and use a model we already have," Sandy said, discouraged.

"How about Susan Overland?" Lydia asked, thumbing through the models' information cards.

"She looks too much like a teen-ager," Sandy objected. "It has to be someone with a clear, bright face, someone who looks good with a minimum of makeup. The lights tend to give the girls a hard appearance anyway, so we have to be careful in our selection."

"There's Margaret Sullivan," Lydia said. "She'd make a beautiful bride."

"Yeah. She'd be perfect. But I had her scheduled to model an outfit right before the finale. We'd have to juggle the lineup."

"Is it worth it?"

"Of course. I want this show to go right," Sandy said with determination. "It's the first one I've coordinated. It's just that I hate to get fifteen models all out-of-sorts at the last minute. You'd be surprised how they can complain. Some of them think they're prima donnas."

"Yeah, I've met that type. They always complain because they're not on the runway long enough, the clothes don't show off their figures just right and the commentator doesn't say enough about them personally."

"Fortunately, we got some of the real pros this time," Sandy said, leaning on the counter, her eyes flitting over the bridal dresses hanging in their clear plastic bags along the far wall. Her gaze returned to Lydia. "They're delightful to work with. They never complain, wear anything we ask them to, show up on time, do their job and thank us for using them.

"But the agency ran in a few new ones on us, and they can be a real pain. One girl had a fit because we wanted her to wear yellow. She said it made her skin sallow."

"What did you do?"

"I told her to wear it or forget about the show," Sandy said firmly.

"And?"

"She poked her bottom lip out, but she's going to wear it."

"I wouldn't have your job," Lydia commented. "It's bad enough dealing with all the problems in this department every day. Frankly, I don't like conflicts and squabbles. If I didn't need the money, I'd stay home and hibernate where there's peace and quiet. But . . ." she sighed, "when you have to work to support yourself, you do what you have to."

"It's a challenge to make everything run smoothly, but I like it," Sandy said. "I'd be bored to death at home. There's something about the excitement of this place that keeps my adrenalin pumping. Every morning I come to work knowing there's going to be something during the day to test my mettle. I look forward to that. It's what keeps me coming back. I like the responsibility, the feeling that my decisions affect others. There's a certain sense of power that feeds some deep need in me. I could never stay home. I'd wither up and die."

Lydia looked at Sandy and smiled. "It's obvious you like what you do. You're so good at it."

"Thanks."

Just then, a messenger from Van Helmut's office

hurried up to them and handed a slip of paper to Sandy. It was a directive; Carl wanted to see her in his office.

"Gotta run," she told Lydia. "Go ahead and fit Margaret Sullivan in the bride's dress."

Lydia nodded.

Sandy was ushered into Carl's office. He sat behind his desk, leafing through some papers.

She cleared her throat.

Carl looked up, stared at her a moment, then spoke. "We have a minor problem, but I'm sure you can handle it. Sit down." His blue eyes glittered with something resembling a challenge.

Sandy took a seat.

"Seems there's been a mix-up in the reservations for the style show," he said, looking right at her.

"What kind of mix-up?"

"Somehow, the girls who were handling the calls overbooked. We have to seat an extra twenty-five people."

"But that's not possible!" Sandy protested. "We've used every inch of available space now. There's not room for one more chair in the Royale Room."

"You'll have to find the room," Carl said sternly. "I will not have Van Helmut's disappoint twenty-five women who have made reservations for our spring fashion show."

Sandy was taken aback by Carl's brusqueness. It was almost as if he really cared what happened. If he was only filling in for his father, what did it matter to him if a handful of people had to be turned down?

"You're asking the impossible," Sandy protested.

"Impossibility exists only in your mind," Carl

said, his voice like a razor. "You can accomplish anything you set your mind to. I want twenty-five additional places set up at the fashion show. Now, can you handle that, or can you not?" His voice said there was no room for further argument.

"Yes, I can handle it," she said coldly. She wondered bitterly how she could have been attracted to this man, even for an instant. He was hard beneath his handsome exterior, maybe even brutal. Was he anything like Roland? She shuddered at the thought and brushed it from her mind.

"Good, I knew you could," Carl said. "Now, to another matter. In the finale, the bride is to carry real flowers. You are to order them from Flowers Unlimited. You have authority to sign for all expenses under a thousand dollars. Anything over that, see me for approval."

"Yes, sir," Sandy replied mechanically.

Carl recited a list of additional orders, which Sandy dutifully noted, then he dismissed her.

Fuming, she left his office. He was a cold, heartless man. He had ordered her to make room for an additional twenty-five people for the fashion show without so much as one consideration for the trouble it would cause her. Where was she going to find space? No matter what the logistics, she was determined to squeeze those extra bodies in somehow. She was equal to any challenge Carl Van Helmut issued her. There was no way she was going to let that man get the best of her!

That afternoon, Sandy drove to the Royale Room to check the progress of the preparations. The 100-foot runway stretched from the back of the long room almost to the other end. It formed a giant "T" with its side runway perpendicular to the main leg.

Workmen hammered noisily as they put the finishing touches on the platform.

Sandy looked around the large room with its brocade wallpaper. Coming from a side room, she saw the foreman of the crew, Abel Chapa.

"Abel," she called, motioning to him with her forefinger. He adjusted his apron with its several pockets for nails, pushed a small cap to the back of his head and strolled over to her.

"Howdy, Miz Carver," he drawled. Sandy smiled at his pronunciation of the word "Miss." She had long ago become accustomed to the twang of some of the Texans in Houston. But there was always something amusing about the use of the word "Miz," which could stand for either "Miss" or "Mrs." It was not in any way related to the "Ms." coined by the women's movement, rather it was a lazy, easy way of avoiding distinguishing between two similar words. Sandy thought of it as a mark of the slower, more relaxed style of Texas.

"Hi, Abel," Sandy smiled. "Looks like the construction is moving right along."

Abel flashed her a toothless grin. He was a small, wiry man. "Yes, ma'am, it's moving pretty smooth."

"I hate to bring this up at the last minute like this, Abel," Sandy said, "but I've got a problem. I sure hope you can help me with it."

"Lay it out for me, ma'am, and I'll see what I can do."

"We need to add twenty-five spaces for seating for the fashion show."

Abel scratched his head. "I don't rightly see how we can do that, ma'am," he drawled.

"I don't either, but we're going to have to find the space somehow." Sandy stood firm.

"Do ya want me to shorten the runway?" Abel asked, frowning. "It'd be a heap of work, but we could do it."

"Only as a last resort. Come on, let's check this arrangement out and see if there's any way we can seat twenty-five additional people without making such a drastic change."

Sandy and Abel spent an hour rearranging chairs, counting and trying to move chairs closer together along the tables edging the runway. By moving the commentator's stand closer to the back wall, adding additional tables in the space and putting two small tables at the far end of the room beyond the end of the runway, they managed to accomplish their goal.

When they were through, Sandy sighed. "I never thought we'd make it," she said heavily. "Just one more complication to throw me behind schedule."

"I sure hope that's the last change in the seating," Abel said. "They's no way we could seat one more person."

"As it is, somebody may have to sit on somebody else's lap," Sandy said wryly.

Abel looked at her blankly.

"Only teasing," she reassured him. At least she was able to maintain a sense of humor in spite of the pressure. She wondered why, the more pressure she was under, the more she felt like joking.

The next day Sandy spent most of her time in the alterations department. The models tried on each fashion, had it tucked in and hemmed up to fit and matched accessories to go with each outfit.

When most of the details were taken care of, Sandy held a meeting with the girls. They all sat on the floor. Scraps of material were scattered around. The sewing machines were silent. Racks of clothes bordered the room. Sandy stood in the center of the group, referring to her handwritten notes.

"For some of you, this is quite familiar," she began. "You've modeled for us before and know our regulations. However, for those of you who are new, I want to make it clear what we expect of you."

Everyone settled quietly into a comfortable position and looked at Sandy.

"First, our rehearsal will be Thursday night. Please be at the Royale Room at 6:30, ready to walk through at 6:45."

A hand shot up. "I don't go on until last," a model said. "Do I have to be there at 6:30?"

"Yes. We'll have a brief meeting before we start, and I want everyone there to hear instructions."

The model shot a slightly disgusted look at another girl on the floor but said nothing.

Anger welled up in Sandy. "You are being well paid for every minute of your time," she said in a brittle tone. "Be on time and give us our money's worth."

"There will be no gum chewing. Please keep in mind that we want a different look for each category of clothes. We'll begin with casual, advance to daytime, then after five, on to evening, and finish with the bridal showing. If you have hair that can be worn in different styles, change it between fashions. You experienced models know that you provide your own hosiery. Please see that you match tones with the outfit you are modeling. You also make up your own faces and are responsible for your hair looking its best. I expect professionalism throughout the show. Remember you are an example to the newer girls, and they are looking to you to know what it means to be a professional model. I want everyone to cooperate in the dressing room and help the show run smoothly. We have seventy-five fashions to show, forty-five minutes to show them, so you're going to have to keep things moving. Are there any questions?"

"Who's going to commentate?"

"Sheila Powers," Sandy said, wishing she had been able to get someone else. But there were too many details to handle to worry about that matter now.

Several of the experienced models frowned. One said, "You know she rushes us. She talks too fast and tries to hurry us off the runway before we've had a chance to show the fashion off completely."

"I'll take care of that," Sandy said. "You just be there and do your job. Leave the rest to me, OK?"

The model nodded mutely.

"The next thing is about the clothes. Each of you is personally responsible for each fashion you are assigned. Our policy is to offer you a twenty-five-percent discount on anything you wear that you want to buy after the show. What you don't buy, you must return to the proper department in perfect condition. So be careful when you're dressing. Don't rip out any seams or get makeup on the garment."

"What if I'm careful, but something happens to the dress anyway?" asked one of the younger girls.

"I'm sorry, but you're still responsible. That's the way it is," Sandy said firmly.

She went on. "Do not remove the tags from the clothes. See that they are tucked in where they don't show while you're on the runway. Also, I expect each of you to wear arm shields to protect the garments from perspiration. Your underwear is your responsibility. Have I overlooked anything?"

"Is the music any good?" a girl asked.

"That depends on what you like," Sandy answered. "We have music with an upbeat tempo and a happy swing. It should lift you and make you want to bounce down that runway with a smile on your face. Remember to look happy. You're just a mannequin as far as the audience is concerned, a human clothes hanger, so remember to exude a little personality to make your fashion sparkle. The way you walk, turn and handle yourself can make or break a style."

The meeting adjourned, and Sandy met with the girl assigned to fill out the form on the lineup. Margaret Sullivan's name had to be marked out and moved around to leave her time to change into the bridal dress for the finale.

Each girl was assigned a number in the show, her garment and accessories were listed beside her name and the section she was to model in was noted.

Then Sandy made sure the individual placards, taped on the wall next to each model's assigned table space, were filled out properly. The girl's name, the date, the show, the model's place in the lineup, each outfit and all accessories were detailed on the card to serve as a guide.

Back in the alterations room, Sandy checked individual garments to see that hems had been taped up snugly and that alterations were hand sewn with long stitches to make them easy to remove without leaving any telltale signs.

It was late, and Sandy was tired. Her shift had been over for some time, but still she checked the details that had to be attended to in order to run a successful style show.

She was leaving the alterations room when she almost bumped into Carl. Her hands were full of notes, reminding her of countless odd jobs she still had left to do. She was sorting through them as she strode swiftly out of the room. Suddenly, she stopped short, just inches from him. Animosity jolted through her. He was the last person she wanted to see at the moment. Every time she was around him, he found some way to goad her into a fit of pique.

"You're working late, aren't you?" he asked. He planted his feet firmly apart, as if ready to conduct the first round of the Inquisition. His tone was accusing.

"What do you expect?" she snapped. "I can't run a fashion show long distance. I have to be here to see that things are done."

"You could assign someone else to take care of some of the details," he said.

She looked him directly in the face. His heavy eyebrows were arched in what she interpreted as an expression of disdain.

"I could if I didn't care whether those details were handled properly," she rebutted sourly.

"You don't trust anybody, do you?" he asked pointedly.

"Why should I? No one has as much at stake in this fashion show as I do. If I don't see that my directions are carried out to the letter, who will? You gave me this responsibility, and I accepted it. Now, are you going to tell me how to coordinate the entire show?" She still hadn't resolved her anger about the additional twenty-five seats.

"My, testy this evening, aren't we?" he remarked condescendingly. "I think you've been working too hard."

"Mr. Van Helmut," Sandy replied cooly, drawing

herself up to her full five-foot-three, "I would hardly call myself testy." Her large brown eyes flashed with anger, but her tone was even. "True, I am working under quite a strain right now, but I can handle it. I assure you, I would not have taken this job had there been any question in my mind of my ability to handle it."

"No, I'm sure you wouldn't have," Carl replied, his voice low and soft. The superior edge had melted from his tone. He sounded almost human, as if he understood how she felt.

She was bewildered by his sudden change in attitude. "I—I'm sorry," she said. "I didn't mean to run off at the mouth like that." It was an apology, but it was offered with a certain reserve in her heart.

"Are you finished for the day?" he asked.

Sandy sighed. "Yeah, I think so. I guess I do need to get home and get some rest."

"I'm just leaving. I'll drive you home." It was more an order than an offer. Should she refuse?

She looked at him standing in front of her, his tall frame blocking out everything beyond him. It had been years since she had been alone with a man, just the two of them isolated from the protection of other people. She had avoided such a situation at all costs.

"No, thank you," she replied. "I have my own car."

"Then come to the coffee shop with me for something to drink. I want to talk to you."

"Now?"

"Yes."

"All right." Sandy shrugged.

She strode along beside him. When they reached the door, he held it for her and let her pass ahead of him. The coffee shop was deserted. Carl brought two cups of coffee to the table, set one in front of her and took the seat opposite her.

They sipped the hot liquid, looking over their cups momentarily at each other. Something in Carl's look stung her. She averted her gaze.

"Well?" she asked. "What did you want to talk about? It sounded like something specific." She looked down at her cup. Slowly, she stirred it with a miniature swizzle stick.

"What do you know about Julia French?" Carl asked.

"Julia?" Sandy looked up, surprised.

"Yes, I understand you and she are good friends."

"That's right. Are you considering her for a promotion or something?"

"No."

"Then may I ask why you want to know about her?"

"She's been seeing my younger brother, Brut."

"And you want to find out if she's good enough for him, is that it?" Sandy asked icily.

"Not exactly. Brut's a widower. He was devastated when his wife died. I just don't want to see him get hurt again."

"I understand," Sandy said more softly. "But he's grown. I'm sure he can look out for himself. And Julia's a fine person. She's reliable, dependable, honest and independent. Brut would be lucky to get her."

"I can see you're very loyal to her," Carl said.

"Not without good reason," Sandy countered. "She's the kind of person it's easy to be loyal to."

"Does she play the field?" Carl asked.

"That's the kind of question you'll have to ask her yourself," Sandy replied aloofly.

"What about you?" Carl asked, his blue eyes glittering. "Do you play the field?"

An invisible hand squeezed Sandy around the throat. Her breath came in short snatches. A metal gate clanked down on her emotions.

"I don't discuss my private life," she said frostily. "Now, Mr. Van Helmut, was there anything else?"

Carl shot her a disappointed frown. "You're strictly business, aren't you?" he asked.

"That's what I was hired for," she replied coolly. "I try to do my job. If you'll check my record, I think you'll find nothing but good reports about my work."

"Yes, that's true, but even in business there's room for human emotion. We deal with people every day, and each one of them is a creature of feelings. The more we recognize that, the better we can serve the public."

Sandy stared at Carl silently. Was he giving her a lecture?

"Do you have complaints about how I handle customers?" Sandy asked pointedly.

"No, not at all."

"I didn't think so. I learned the business from the ground floor up. When I was at the candy counter, I had a lot of time to observe the women in the other departments around me."

"And what did you learn?"

"A lot. Customers like that personal touch. And in this store they look for quality. The important thing is to figure out who holds the purse strings. In the junior department, for instance, it's the mother. So I appeal directly to her when I try to sell up. I suggest to her the matching items for any garment her daughter is considering. But because of the rebellious nature of the teen-ager, I must sound as if I hardly expect the daughter to like it. It works."

"You catch on fast, don't you?"

"You bet I do," Sandy said confidently. "I learned a long time ago that no one is going to look out for me, so I better look out for myself. I observed the most successful sales personnel in the store, listened to your father with his trite but true observations, such as, 'A dog today will be a dog tomorrow,' and learned the basics of retailing."

Carl smiled. "I bet I've heard that one a million times."

"It's kind of corny, but your father knows what he's doing. He must have to have kept this store so successful. I figured out the way to the top is to listen to winners. If you associate with losers and believe them, you become a loser, too." Sandy's voice was embroidered with bitterness.

"I can't imagine you ever being a loser," Carl said, eyeing her speculatively, a strange gleam in his eyes.

"Good," she said, relieved that her past didn't show in her face. "Now, if there's nothing else, I *am* tired and would like to get home." She gave him a questioning glance.

"Thanks for joining me," he said, rising.

I didn't know I had any choice, she thought wryly, but she said nothing.

The Thursday night rehearsal at the Royale Room began at precisely 6:45. Before the actual run-through began, Sandy gave the models their last-minute instructions. They were seated along one of the dining tables, which looked bare and cheap without the linen tablecloth that would eventually cover it. The large room echoed softly with the sounds of chairs being moved into place and last-minute adjustments to the sound system.

Sandy stood at the end of the table, a clipboard in her hand. She glanced at her notes.

"Is Martha Johnson here?" she asked.

A hand went up.

"Martha, we're changing your after-five fashion to the casual section. It would fit either category, and we have one too many outfits in casuals. See me after my announcements, and I'll tell you where we'll squeeze you in."

Martha nodded and smiled.

"I've checked the dressing room, which is behind these double doors, and there is no carpet. So we'll have a roll of masking tape backstage. Use it to tape the bottom of any shoes from the store that you wear. If you forget, and scratch the soles of the shoes, you've bought them."

"Can we wear our own shoes if they're the same color as the ones we're to model?" asked one of the girls.

"Only if they look new and the commentator doesn't mention them in her commentary."

Sandy glanced at the questioner to see if the model understood. The girl nodded.

"Please, no food or drinks in the dressing room tomorrow during the show. Since you'll be modeling for a luncheon, you'll miss your own lunch, but we do not provide anything for you to eat. Our main concern is not to get anything on the clothes.

"Our rehearsal will be conducted without wearing any of the fashions, so you're to imagine you have on what you'll be modeling tomorrow. That will give me an idea of how you plan to show the garment. Are there any questions?"

There was silence, so Sandy ushered the women into the dressing room and headed for the speaker's stand on a high platform at the front of the room.

"Is Sheila here yet?" Sandy asked an assistant who was stringing an electrical cord across the carpeted floor.

The assistant shrugged and worked on.

"I knew I was going to have trouble with her," Sandy grumbled to herself.

"Hey, Claudia," Sandy called to another assistant, "have you seen Sheila Powers? She's supposed to commentate. We're ready to start."

"I haven't seen her," Claudia said.

"Then I need you. Come here, will you?"

Claudia put down the balloons she was blowing up for table decorations and approached.

Sandy handed her a list of the run of the show.

"Will you stand by the dressing-room door and make sure the models are ready when their name is called? I'm going to have to fill in for Sheila."

"Sure," Claudia said. "Glad to."

Sandy ground her teeth in frustration but smiled. There was no point in taking out her anger on Claudia.

She climbed up on the speaker's stand, laid out her pages of commentary and looked around the room. The long runway stretched out before her; the same height as the tabletops. The models were in the dressing room, the sound technician sat near the tape recorder and several people milled around, working on decorations. Everything was in order, but Sheila Powers still had not put in an appearance.

"Music," Sandy called out, trying to camouflage the irritation in her voice.

A swinging, lively recording blared out of the speakers.

"That's too loud," Sandy said. "You'll have to keep the volume down."

The technician twisted a knob, and the sound subsided.

Sandy read the introduction to the style show and had commentated the first three fashions when Sheila Powers rushed through the door at the back of the room.

She hurried to the front, climbed the speaker's stand and smiled sweetly at Sandy.

"Sorry I'm late," she said breathlessly, "but it was unavoidable."

"You will be here on time tomorrow, won't you?" Sandy asked stiffly.

"Well, naturally," Sheila said, as if the mere possibility of being tardy was beyond her belief.

"I'm counting on it," Sandy said, pushing the sheets of commentary toward the other side of the stand as she turned to go.

Sandy hurried to the dressing-room door, took charge of ushering the models in and out and eyed them as they walked briskly down the runway.

Just then, a tall, blond figure appeared in the doorway at the back of the room.

Sandy drew in her breath. What was Carl Van Helmut doing here? Didn't he trust her to run things?

She hadn't allowed herself to think about him since their conversation over coffee the previous day. She had refused to speculate on the real reason for his wanting to talk to her. She had pushed aside her feelings about him. But now, seeing him in person, she could no longer deny her curiosity. Why had he asked her about her love life and if she played the field? Was he asking just to make small talk, or was he genuinely interested?

Why did his presence arouse in her strong emotions she didn't understand?

Carl's eyes swung around the room. Then, he took a seat at one of the tables and watched the proceedings.

Sandy didn't approve of his spying on her. She knew what she was doing. The fashion show would be a success, and much of it would be due to her attention to detail. Carl knew she was competent at anything she tackled. So why did he attend?

Ripples of disapproval radiated through her. But she said nothing and turned her attention to her work.

"Mandy, remember the pace is upbeat," Sandy instructed a model about to ascend the runway. "Be peppy up the stairs."

"I'll try," she said, "but with my peers watching me, I get a little nervous. I think they're all criticizing me." She motioned to the gaggle of women peering through the dressing-room doors. She laughed. "Tomorrow afternoon at the luncheon will be different. An audience really turns me on."

"Then just give it your best shot tonight," Sandy said. She knew how unnerving it was to be in the spotlight. As she mused, she eyed Carl at the back of the room.

"Hey, Abel," Sandy called out, "what about the lights around the platform?"

The little man, who had been hunched over something he was working on, straightened. He shot

Sandy his toothless grin and waved to her. He connected a cord, and flashing lights blinked on. They were synchronized with the beat of the music and ran the entire length of the runway.

"That's it," Sandy called approvingly.

The rest of the rehearsal went according to plan. Sheila talked too fast, Sandy spoke to her about it and the pace of the show moved at the right tempo.

Carl strolled up and down by the tables and finally approached Sandy.

"Hello," she said coolly. "Checking things out?"

"Yes," he said.

Spots of anger turned her cheeks pink.

He went on. "I wanted to check the layout before I came with the diamond necklace tomorrow. You can't be too careful with something like that."

"Oh," Sandy said, momentarily relenting. A burst of embarrassment shot through her. Then, suspicion took its place. Was it really the necklace he was worried about, or was it her ability to coordinate the fashion show? This was the annual spring showing of all the latest styles from Van Helmut's department store. It was also one of the social highlights of the Houston scene. Fashionable women from all over the sprawling metropolis paid the inflated luncheon price every year not only to see but to be seen. This was the fashion show to attend, the one everyone talked about for weeks afterward.

Sandy realized every detail counted. Her patrons were highly critical. They were a jaded bunch of women after the many style shows they had attended. Impressing them with the proper music, decorations and selections of clothes worn by professional models would take a stroke of genius.

But Sandy felt herself equal to the task. She had

handled most of the details herself, and she knew quality. This show was sure to be a hit, if she had anything to do with it. It rubbed her the wrong way that Carl Van Helmut might question her competence.

"Besides, Father wanted to know how things were going. This will be the first fashion show he's ever missed," Carl said.

"How is your father?" Sandy asked.

"As feisty as ever, but a little scared, I'd say. Nothing has ever kept him down before. But the doctor put the fear of God in him this time. He said the phlebitis could kill him if he didn't follow orders. So, he's staying in bed as instructed."

Sandy had a hard time picturing the robust, hearty Otto Van Helmut lying in a sickbed. He was such an obstinate old man. He seemed so in control of his own destiny. It was difficult to imagine a man like that helpless, having to depend on others for anything.

While Sandy often disagreed with the senior Van Helmut on matters of detail, such as displays for her own department and the authority to hire and fire in her own department, there was no denying his merchandising acumen.

She eyed Carl momentarily, wondering just how much like his father he was. He seemed to possess that same rare quality of strength and determination to make life bend to his will. Yet, when he had first taken charge of the store, he had refused to make any decisions on his own.

Sandy knew so little about Carl. His main trait seemed to be a zeal for goading her. And he certainly didn't mind pointedly telling her what he thought of her personality!

What did it matter to her what kind of person he was, she thought, surprised at where her thoughts were taking her. She could care less. It was strictly a business relationship, one that would most likely end when Otto Van Helmut recuperated. And then Carl would fade into the background, going back to wherever he had been before he had been thrust onto the scene in his father's place. Vaguely, she wondered where that was. Then she mentally chided herself for such foolish thoughts.

"How long do you think he'll be away from the store?" Sandy asked.

"That's hard to tell."

"Is he eager to come back?"

"He was at first, but lately he seems to be enjoying having a little time off. However, he questions me about everything that's going on. My mother would like to have him home as long as she can keep him."

Sandy wanted to ask Carl how he felt about running his father's store, but she felt that question was too personal. Besides, she hesitated to tread on somebody else's private life, especially when that somebody was a man. The farther her distance from men, the more secure she felt.

"Well, guess I better wrap up the rehearsal," Sandy said, excusing herself.

Carl nodded. As she walked away, she felt his eyes following her. There had been nothing intimate in their conversation, yet Sandy was left with the feeling that Carl had looked deeply into her soul in some special way that left her shaken.

Every time she was around him, she was disturbingly aware of his presence. It was not a feeling she wanted to admit. She had no room in her life for men, especially one who was cold and calculating.

Sandy brushed aside thoughts of Carl and returned her attention to the show.

Everything would run according to schedule at the show, Sandy reassured herself. She'd see to it. She'd show Carl Van Helmut just what she was made of. He might not trust her abilities, but she knew she could handle anything she tackled.

The rest of the rehearsal ran like clockwork, down to the showing of the last fashion before the finale.

Suddenly, one of the models hurried up to her.

"Miss Carver, Margaret's sick."

"What do you mean, sick?" Sandy asked. Tension snapped in the air.

"She began to feel bad a while ago, but she didn't say anything. She thought she'd be all right. But she got to feeling worse and worse. She's in the ladies' room right now, throwing up."

"Oh, no," Sandy groaned. "She's supposed to model the bridal gown. Where is she?"

"Come on, I'll show you."

Sandy followed the model down the hallway and into the ladies' room. Margaret was in one of the stalls, making awful retching sounds. Sandy opened the stall door. The girl was bent over, her face almost white, her eyes watery but her cheeks scarlet.

"Margaret, what is it?" Sandy asked.

"I don't know," the girl said weakly. "I feel awful. Maybe it's the flu."

Sandy reached out a hand. Margaret's skin felt like fire. "You're burning up with fever!"

"What'll we do about the bridal dress?" the other girl asked.

"I'll handle it," Sandy said firmly. "Just get Margaret home. She needs to be in bed."

"Oh, Miss Carver," Margaret blubbered. "I'm so sorry. You were counting on me."

"You can't help it, Margaret," Sandy said. "We'll manage."

"I know you can replace me," she said tearfully, "but I've exposed everyone in the place to whatever I have. What if they all come down with it?"

"That's not very likely," Sandy said.

But in the back of her mind, she knew she was lying. She had no idea what kind of illness Margaret had or how contagious it could be. If it was confined to Margaret, Sandy could hustle to replace this one model. But if it spread to the other girls, the entire show could be ruined!

Chapter Four

"Remember, girls, no smoking," Sandy said to the assembled group of models. "The clothes pick up the odor of smoke. Now, does anyone have any special problems before we start?"

Inwardly Sandy winced. She was too tired to cope with anything else, but she had assumed this responsibility willingly, and she'd see it through.

She could hardly believe what had transpired since the night before. As soon as the rehearsal ended, she had got on the phone to the modeling agency. It had taken quite some time to track down the director at that time of night. Then, she had asked for a replacement for Margaret. The girl she was finally assigned was perfect for the bridal outfit, but she was shorter than Margaret, and all the clothes Margaret had been scheduled to wear had to be hemmed up.

Sandy called the alterations lady close to midnight and had her on the job first thing in the morning. At the moment, the woman was huddled down near the floor, shortening a dress the stand-in was wearing.

The dressing room was crowded with women. Long ago, all models had been size eight. But buyers these days demanded more realistic models, and there were the tiny ones to show the petite clothes and one size eighteen to display the large woman's fashions. Today's models ranged in height from just over five feet to the six-footer, so alterations were an accepted part of any style show.

"The flowers for the bride aren't here yet," said Vergie Johnson. Sandy had selected Vergie to assist her during the morning.

"Call the florist and demand they get them here immediately," Sandy said firmly. "Let me know what they say."

"Okay, I'll be right back."

"Does each model have a dresser?" Sandy asked. "You're not going to have much time between changes, so locate your dresser now and be sure you know who is assigned to you."

"I don't know who mine is," said one woman.

"Your name?" Sandy asked.

"Pamela Martin."

Sandy looked down her list. "Pamela, Mildred Bowers has been assigned to help dress you. Is Mildred here?"

A woman raised her hand. "Here I am," she said.

"Are you new?" Sandy asked.

Mildred nodded.

"Do you understand what you're to do?"

"Help her get dressed, right?"

"Yes, but there's more to it than that. See that list of fashions taped over the table over there?" Sandy pointed to one of the many tables bordering the room. On each there was an array of makeup, some of it spilling out of overnight bags or makeup cases. Hair dryers, rollers, mascara tubes, powder puffs, curling irons, nail polish, combs and brushes, hair spray and assorted other items covered the tables. "On each list you'll find the fashion for your particular model plus all her accessories. While she is on the runway, you are to get her next garment off the hanger and gather all her accessories. This is a fast-paced show. As soon as the model reaches the door, she'll begin running. You see to it that her dress gets unzipped or unbuttoned, that she gets into her next fashion as quickly as possible and that what she has just taken off is hung back on the rack properly. Okay?"

Mildred nodded. "Got you," she said, winking confidently.

"Good. We have thirty minutes before the show starts. This is the only leisurely change you'll have. Remember to use your arms on the runway and exude a lot of personality. Smile, make eye contact with the audience, but show your fashion and get off the stage as quickly as possible. When we have the finale, with everyone on stage, don't bunch up. Spread yourselves out evenly over the entire length of the runway. Break a leg!" She ended her speech with the theatrical equivalent of "good luck."

The models strode to their assigned tables, which were flanked with racks of clothes. In the center of the room was a full-length mirror propped against two chairs. This was not the ideal dressing room, but a large, portable wall divider separating the male models from the women made the large area serviceable.

Although Sandy had coordinated the entire show, she had not been responsible for the men's fashions. The head of the men's department always took charge of them.

"Miss Carver," said one of the models. Sandy turned to face a tall woman with frosted blond hair and a heavily made-up face. "They sent me the wrong size shoes. I wear an eight. These are seven and a half."

Sandy glanced into the shoe box at the red pumps. "Can you wear them anyway?" she asked. "You'll be on stage such a short time."

"I guess so," the woman winced. "At least I'll give it a try."

"Good show," Sandy said encouragingly. She gritted her teeth and wondered what else would go wrong. Fashion shows never ran smoothly. There were the inevitable foul-ups, last minute mistakes and unexpected obstacles. They added a certain drama to the proceedings that made Sandy's adrenalin flow and gave her an exciting, thrilling feeling. In spite of that, she'd prefer the operation to run as planned. However, she knew that was not to be, and she was prepared to handle whatever came up. That was part of her job.

There was a rising hubbub of activity and noise as the dressing for the first run got under way.

"Let's keep it down a little bit," Sandy said over the din. "Our customers will hear you."

The conversations subsided somewhat as dresses were snatched from racks, makeup completed and hair recombed and fluffed out.

Sandy stood near the double doors to the Royale Room, just to one side of the divider between the men and women. Then, a tall figure came through the doors. His thick blond hair shone in the lights that swept over him as the doors parted. His face fell in shadows, casting intriguing patches of darkness over his features, hiding his expression.

For a moment, Sandy was spellbound. A model broke the magic moment when she hurried up to Sandy, a troubled expression on her face.

"Somebody overlooked pressing this shawl," she said. "I can't wear it wrinkled like this."

Sandy was disturbingly aware of Carl's presence. He was eyeing her to see what she would do. Normally, she would not have given a moment's thought to whether she was prepared to handle the situation. But with him scrutinizing her critically, she experienced a moment of tension.

"I brought a travel iron," she said. "It's in that blue bag over there."

"Thank goodness," the model said with a sigh and scurried off to take care of the problem

"Having the usual eleventh-hour crises?" Carl asked, his blue eyes sparkling.

He enjoyed watching her squirm, she thought belligerently. A lightning bolt of anger shot through her.

"I can handle them," she replied confidently. Involuntarily, her eyes trailed down from his head to his broad shoulders. He wore a turtleneck sweater, a checkered sport coat and tan trousers. He was much more handsome than any of the male models lined up for the show and showed off his clothes with an air of cosmopolitan sophistication. He walked with an easy, confident stride.

Sandy tore her gaze from him. She refused to allow herself to think about Carl Van Helmut as a man. He was merely her business superior, and a temporary one at that.

"Is this your first time backstage at a style show?" she asked.

"No, I've been to many," he said. "I was involved in the business a number of years back."

So that's why he knew how to take charge of everything. Sandy knew very little about Carl's background and how much he had been in touch with the Van Helmut enterprises. It was clear he knew something about merchandising. He had stepped into his father's shoes without a bit of trouble. Since he at first had refused to make any decisions contrary to his father's wishes, she had wondered if he knew anything about the store. But it had become increasingly clear that he knew the workings of the store inside and out.

Vergie rushed up behind Sandy. "The flowers for the bride are on their way," she said. "The florist assured me they'd be here within the next twenty minutes."

"They better be," Sandy said determinedly.

Carl arched an eyebrow but said nothing.

"How long until we start?" Vergie asked.

"Twenty minutes," Sandy said, looking at her watch.

"Then they should be here just as we begin the show."

"That will be soon enough, if they make it," Sandy said.

"And if they don't?" Vergie asked.

"Let me worry about that."

"What about the diamond necklace?" Vergie asked.

Sandy turned to Carl and shot him a questioning look.

"I have it," he said. "I'll place it on the model just before she steps through the doors. I'll also remove it when she returns. You didn't tell her she was wearing real diamonds, did you?"

"No," Sandy replied. "I did as you asked. I just told her she was to receive her jewelry here at the door. I understand your security precautions."

"I knew you would." His tone was warm.

Sandy looked at him, surprised at the caring quality in his voice. She wanted to speculate inwardly as to what it might mean, but there wasn't time.

"Where's the masking tape?" a model who had come up behind her asked. "Somebody forgot to hem up these pants. I'll have to get the legs shortened before I can wear them."

Sandy turned to the table behind her. On it were various pieces of jewelry, rolls of tape, hair spray, combs and bobby pins. Sandy picked up a roll of tape and bent down to tuck up the excess length of the pants. Carefully, she taped the hem so that the legs matched perfectly.

"Thanks," the model said and disappeared round the divider.

"I lost an earring," came a voice behind the divider.

"I know I'm going to get out there and fall flat on my face," said another.

"Just think how sympathetic the audience will be," said the first voice with a chuckle.

"I had to wear three pairs of hose to get all the

right shades for my outfits," came still another voice. "I'm going to feel like a banana from peeling them off between changes."

"Is it really necessary to match your stockings to your clothes?" asked a voice, obviously one of the dressers.

"It sure is," came the answer. "A professional attends to even the smallest detail."

"Have you been modeling long?" the dresser's voice asked.

"Quite a while. I got out of the business for a few years. I got tired of the hassles. They always called me at the last minute to fill in for somebody, and it was invariably right when I was in the middle of scrubbing the bathroom!" she said, laughing. "But I missed it, so I decided to come back."

Her voice became muffled. Sandy surmised she was pulling something over her head.

Carl tossed Sandy a wry grin. "Do you feel like an eavesdropper?" he asked, indicating the voice floating over the dividing wall.

"I'm used to that kind of talk," she said. "I hear it all the time. If you want to listen in to something, you ought to hear customers in the dressing rooms at the store trying on clothes. Those teen-age girls give away all their secrets."

A model emerged from behind the divider. She flashed Carl a wide smile; her cheeks flushed. "Does this collar go in or out?" she asked, pointing to a rolled collar on a blouse worn under a red blazer.

"Let's try it both ways and see what looks better," Sandy suggested.

The model smoothed the collar down under the jacket and stood for a moment while Sandy eyed her.

"Now the other way," Sandy said.

The girl flipped the collar to the outside and swung her shoulders seductively from side to side, her eyes flirting with Carl.

"Outside looks better," Sandy said coldly. It was disgusting the way the model was making an obvious play for Carl.

"What do you think?" the model said coyly, batting her eyes at Carl.

"The same. Outside looks better."

Obvious disappointment registered on the woman's face. She apparently had hoped for more personal attention from Carl. She gave a little pout and turned and walked back behind the divider to complete her dressing.

"Some designers need to send directions with their creations," Sandy observed.

Carl smiled. His even, straight teeth glistened. For a moment, he seemed human, almost approachable. But Sandy didn't have time to examine her feelings about that instant captured in time by her memory. For now, she'd have to put it aside, only to be able to draw it out later and contemplate what it might mean.

A model came from behind the divider. She held out a hand to Sandy. In it lay a black-fringed false eyelash. "It's a good thing I don't have to look sexy all the time," she said. "I couldn't stand it. Can you help me with this? I can't get it on straight, and my dresser is all thumbs."

"Sure," Sandy said.

She took the eyelash and a tube of glue, spread the sticky substance carefully along the edge and gingerly positioned it on the model's left eye. It took a few minutes to work it into place so that both eyes matched.

"There, I think that's it," she said.

"Thanks."

"Women," Carl chuckled, as the model returned to her dressing area. "You notice none of the men are having problems with little details such as eyelashes. Everything on their side is running like clockwork."

"Is that an indictment?" Sandy asked icily. Was Carl in some way criticizing her?

"Just an observation," he commented.

"We wouldn't have problems like this if it weren't for you men," she said accusingly.

"How so?" He raised an eyebrow.

"If men didn't expect women to look like fashion photos all the time, we wouldn't have to go to such ridiculous lengths to please them."

Carl's eyes swept over Sandy's face. "You look fine to me, and I don't see any signs that you've gone to any ridiculous lengths to look good."

A smoldering ire caught fire in Sandy. Who gave him the right to comment on her looks? Besides, what did he mean by saying she looked "fine"? Was that a slight? Or was it his attempt at a compliment? Whatever it was, she didn't appreciate the personal nature of his observation.

The silence sliced the air into thin, ragged strips.

"You needn't take it so personally," Carl said in a low voice. "Doesn't that chip on your shoulder get awfully heavy? It's one of the largest ones I've ever encountered."

Sandy shot him a defiant look. She started to retort with a sarcastic remark. But then she realized how right he was. He obviously was trying to be humorous in his comments about all the details the women had to take care of. He was not accusing her of incompetence in any way. She had taken offense at his remark without justification.

Should she apologize? Or would that make matters worse?

"My chip gets a little tiresome sometimes," she said with a forced smile. "But I manage to get around somehow."

Carl smiled at her, the skin around his eyes crinkling with amusement. He had tossed out a verbal jest, and she had responded. It was the first time they had laughed together about her protective wall. It frightened her a little bit that they could acknowledge it so openly. Pretending it didn't exist seemed the safest way to keep it intact.

Sheila Powers pushed through the door leading into the Royale Room and smiled at Sandy. "Everything out front looks superb. You've done a great job, Sandy. Mind if I talk to the girls a minute?"

"Of course not. Come on, I'll announce it to them."

It was a relief to get away from Carl. He was stirring up in her a bewildering combination of emotions she wasn't sure she could handle. He was so direct. She preferred a certain amount of subterfuge when it came to her inner feelings about things. She didn't want to let anyone know what she felt. She wore a plastic smile for the benefit of the world, but in her chest beat a tattered heart. It was not something she ever discussed; it was her own personal wound, which had healed, leaving deep scars she tried not to think about.

Sandy called the models to order. Most were dressed for their first walk down the runway. Some were putting on finishing touches of makeup or combing their hair. One girl, with a long mop of thick, wavy hair, was twisting it up under a jaunty cap.

Sheila stood next to Sandy while the room came to a hush. Everyone stopped and settled near the front of the room. Sheila smiled.

"Girls," she said, "I'm very happy to be your commentator. I like to keep the pace moving, but I'll give you plenty of time to show your fashion. If I run out of commentary, I can ad-lib, but I prefer to hold each model to less than a minute on the runway. There will be a drawing for a door prize halfway through the show, so that will give you a little breather to dress for the next segment.

"Rehearsal went just fine, so I'm expecting a good show. Feel free to add personal touches or extra wiggles when you walk. Stay happy. Faces up, cheery. Enjoy."

Sheila held her arms up, palms outstretched, as if giving her own special blessing.

"See you on stage in five minutes," she said.

Sheila picked up the pages of her script from the table behind her and exited.

"Any last-minute problems?" Sandy asked.

"Yes," said a model. "This button on my blazer fell off."

"Do you have to remove the jacket during the show?" Sandy asked.

"Yes."

"Can you put your hand over the spot and keep it covered up if we don't have time to sew it back on?"

"I think so. I'll try."

"Okay. Check with Vergie over here at the side table for needle and thread. But if you don't get it back on, do the best you can."

"It's time to line up," Sandy went on. She called the names of the first group of models and made sure each was in her proper spot.

Then she checked with Vergie, who was standing near the divider.

"Are the bride's flowers here, yet?" Why had she used the florist Carl had suggested? It irritated her to be put in a bind because of him. She should have chosen the florist she wanted to use. But she dared not say anything to Carl about it.

"They just arrived," Vergie said. "I gave them to the model."

"Thank goodness," Sandy sighed. She pushed past the line of models and took her place near the doors opposite Carl, who stood on the other side of the line of women.

The music began. Muffled sounds seeped through the slit in the double doors. It was an upbeat, happy tempo. The sound system sprang to life with Sheila Powers's voice explaining that the theme of the spring collection was golden sunrise.

Sandy looked confidently over the waiting models. She felt a sense of satisfaction. She had done her job well. The last-minute minor calamities she had handled were part of any style show. Nothing had come up that had stumped her; the bride's flowers had arrived at the last minute, they had a replacement for Margaret, everyone had shown up and even Sheila Powers had paced herself well in rehearsal.

Had Sandy known what was to transpire later that afternoon, she wouldn't have felt quite so sure of herself. But since she could not see into the future, she stood at the door calmly, ushering the girls in and out through the double doors, checking her list to see who was next, marking off those who had completed their turn, handling several minor problems and keeping the dressing room organized.

As each model finished her walk down the runway, she hurried backstage, running through the doors, pulling off clothes as she sped by. Sandy alternated between the double doors and the area behind the divider. The male models stood casually to the left of Carl, waiting their turn.

One model stood in line adjusting her clothes. Sandy noticed that the pockets of her pants showed through the fabric. "Tuck your pants pockets up under your knit top," she suggested.

The model smiled, nodded and complied.

"Be sure to check how you look in the back," she told another woman, whose lingerie peeked out from a low cut halter top that was scooped down below her shoulder blades in the back.

"Does anyone have a beige slip?" said a voice behind the divider.

"Here, you can borrow mine," came the reply. "But I'll need it for the next segment."

"My zipper won't zip!" came an irritated voice.

The double doors swung open, and a model rushed in.

"Pin it with this safety pin."

Another model hurried out the doors and toward the runway.

"How did you do?"

"Terrible by my standards," came the reply.

"Next time do a lot of turns."

"I'll fall off the runway."

"Right into a handsome man's arms!"

"Uuuh . . ." several voices cooed together.

"Come on, we don't have time for that," another chuckled.

The doors opened again. Models brushed past each other as one hurried in and the other strode out.

When they got to the evening wear, Carl strode over to Sandy. "Who wears the diamond necklace?" he asked.

Sandy checked her list. "Elizabeth Cavanaugh. That one." She pointed to the model in the plunging black silk dress.

Carl reached into his pocket and pulled out a black velvet cloth. From it he lifted a beautiful diamond necklace. He walked over to Elizabeth, who was standing in line. He spoke to her momentarily. Her eyes sparkled with excitement.

Elizabeth was a gorgeous woman. She was tall. Her large blue eyes were fringed with long lashes. Her willowy shape looked lean and sexy in the tight dress she wore.

Sandy couldn't see Carl's face as he talked with the model. But she couldn't help wondering if there was a sparkle in his eyes, too.

Elizabeth turned, and Carl put his arms around her for a moment to place the necklace over her throat. Something unpleasant shot through Sandy. She couldn't identify the feeling, but she refused to look at Carl and Elizabeth any longer.

Instead, she peeked through the double doors to see what was happening on stage. A male model was sauntering down the runway, showing off a tuxedo and ruffled shirt. The audience was held in rapt attention as the model removed his jacket and held it over his arm. Sandy saw what was going on, but it didn't really register in her brain. Something blocked the impulse going to her mind so that she was only vaguely aware of the scene before her eyes.

Soon Elizabeth walked through the double doors, and Carl stood looking through the slit in the double doors at her. Was he keeping an eye on the necklace, Sandy wondered. Or was it the woman who wore the diamonds he was more interested in?

What difference did it make, anyway, she chided herself. The kind of woman who attracted Carl Van Helmut was no concern of hers.

When Elizabeth returned to the dressing room, Sandy looked away as Carl removed the necklace.

It seemed only minutes until it was time for the bride's dress to be shown. And then the show was over. Everything had fallen into place.

The frantic pace in the dressing room ground to a standstill for a few minutes and the women stood around and discussed the show.

Finally, the girls began dressing in their own clothes and putting away the makeup and assorted accessories that had filled the tables. Sheila Powers came backstage and congratulated everyone. The more demonstrative types hugged each other and agreed to call and chat when they had time.

The customers in the Royale Room slowly filtered out the doors. Waiters arrived to clean the tables of the luncheon dishes and the construction crew began to break down the runway.

Clothes were packed away, shoes returned to boxes, and soon the dressing room was almost deserted.

Sandy stood in the middle of the room watching the last model pack up. She had done it, she thought. She had taken a difficult job and had made a success of it. She had been determined not to let anything stand in her way. Carl Van Helmut might be right in saying she had a chip on her shoulder. But she knew how to get things done. He surely had to recognize that fact. Of all the people he could have chosen for this job, he had picked her.

What did it matter what he thought of her personally? She wasn't trying to win a popularity contest. Her goal was to make a success of herself in the business world. She had just climbed another rung in the ladder. That was reason to be happy.

The last model left, and Sandy checked the room for any items accidentally left behind. Naturally, there were several compacts and a few rollers that had spilled unseen onto the floor. Sandy put them into a bag and gathered her own belongings together on a table.

Just then she heard a footstep behind her. Startled, she turned and faced Carl.

"I thought you left after you got your necklace back," she said. Her heart was pounding from having been surprised.

"As you can see, I hung around," Carl said, approaching her. "I wanted to tell you what a fine job you did. You handled everything like a professional."

"What makes you think I'm not a professional?" Sandy asked.

"I didn't say you weren't. I'm just saying you lived up to what I expected of you."

"Was there some doubt in your mind?" she asked. If he had wondered about her ability, why had he chosen her?

"Not really. But I was watching you to see how you'd stand up under pressure."

Anger and defiance struggled for the upper hand in her emotions. "And did I pass your test?" she asked defensively.

"You know you did . . . almost too well."

She was puzzled. "Wh-what do you mean by that?"

Carl shifted his weight from one foot to another. He paused. A perplexed expression crossed his face. "You're so much in control of yourself. It's almost as if you've turned off your feelings and operate strictly on logic. That's an unusual character trait for a woman."

Sandy's gaze dropped to the concrete floor. It was disturbing to have him talk to her in such a blunt fashion about her emotions.

He went on. "I'd guess you're afraid to let yourself relax."

The hair on the back of her neck prickled. His words hit too close to their target. Her hands felt suddenly clammy.

She was aware that she was alone in the dressing room with Carl. His nearness and their isolation unnerved her. She had to get away.

"It's getting late," she said. "I'd better get things wrapped up here and get back to the store. There are still a lot of details to tend to before this fashion show goes down into the history books."

Blindly she brushed past Carl and headed for the safety of the doors that led into the other room and toward an exit from the hotel.

But she was stopped short by a strong hand. The warm fingers were hard and insistent against her reluctant arm.

"Wh-what do you want?" she stammered. Her eyes were wide with anxiety.

"I want you not to rush off," he said with an easy smile. He released her arm.

At first she felt relieved. But a little flicker of something pleasurable stirred inside her as she looked at him. There was a quality in his voice that broke through some kind of barrier she had lived within—for so long she had forgotten it existed. It had become such an intimate, everyday part of her, she had thought it a natural part of every woman. But now, an opposing force was clamoring for recognition. She didn't know what it was or what to do about it. She only knew it touched off a panic button somewhere in her. She fought to maintain control of her composure.

"But I have so much to do."

"It will keep." He looked at her for a long time, his eyes studying her features.

She blushed. Her throat felt hot. It constricted. What in heaven's name did he want?

"You're really dedicated to your job, aren't you?" he asked.

"Yes."

"I admire you for that. Too many people today want a free ride. Or they expect to graduate from high school and step right into an executive position. But you've worked your way up in the store, learning the business from the bottom up. You're destined to go far."

"I hope so," Sandy replied, relaxing a bit. Now that he was talking about her work, he didn't seem so threatening.

"There's one thing that puzzles me, though."

"What's that?" she asked.

"What makes you tick? What drives Sandy Carver to be the dedicated career woman?"

"Why would you want to know that?" His probing disturbed her. She didn't like it when people asked personal questions about her feelings. Yet he asked in such a genuinely concerned way that she couldn't really rebuff him.

"Curiosity, I guess. I'm sort of a student of human nature. It's a trait I learned from my father. It helped him build a successful business. He figured out how to please customers, learned to appeal to the finer, more refined side of their humanity and built a reputation for concern for the people who walk through the doors of his institution. He really cares about people, about their needs and their feelings. Yet he's tough. He can be hard when he has to be hard. I've seen some of the same strength in you. But is the softness there, too? Sometimes it's hard to detect, like in my father. But it exists. I'm trying to figure out if you also have a softer side."

Sandy clenched her fists with a stubborn determination. She would not allow Carl Van Helmut to worm his way into her emotions. She had no room for him there. "I'll leave that for you to decide," she said.

"And I know just the way to find out," he said huskily.

Before the implied threat had time to register, Carl reached out and took Sandy in his arms. He pulled her to him. His chest was hard under his shirt. He felt warm and human, manly and powerful. His muscles tightened as her breasts flattened out against him.

At first, Sandy stood rigid. She felt like a statue suspended in time. Her mind leaped outside herself, and she refused to believe this was happening to her.

A man had not touched her for years. The unexpected suddenness of being thrust into Carl's arms was like a bolt of electroshock therapy.

Before she could stop him, Carl gathered her close, pulling her face toward his with a hand on the back of her head. For a moment he paused, looking questioningly into her eyes. The warm breath from his nostrils seemed to melt a portion of her icy reserve.

Carl parted his lips. Her eyes were drawn to his mouth. It was so close, so very real, so very masculine. Her heart hammered rapidly.

Then his mouth bore down on hers. His lips were moist and warm, soft, full, probing and gentle. Slowly, he worked his mouth on hers. He seemed larger than life, engulfing her in his embrace, sweeping her into his arms and holding her there, a willing prisoner of his desire.

For a moment, Sandy let her emotions rule. It felt so wonderful to be kissed. Her lips tingled with pleasure. She let her muscles relax and became fluid and limp in Carl's arms.

Whether she was willing to admit it or not, there was a special magic between a man and a woman attracted to each other, a magic that came to fruition only when the two made physical contact.

Carl sent a shiver down her spine by rubbing the fingers of one hand down her arm. Then he gently stroked her hair and turned her head to increase the pressure of the kiss.

A deep longing overcame Sandy. Suddenly, she found herself returning Carl's kiss, working her mouth on his, inwardly sighing. In the deep recesses of her mind, she heard the passionate beat of distant jungle rhythms. They grew louder and louder until their beat pulsated through her entire body.

For a moment, she forgot who she was and where she was. She was woman and he was man, and they were enjoying the fruits of their differences. Nothing else mattered. Her attention was focused on the heavenly yearning building in her. All time and space dissolved into one sphere of meaningless infinity. There was only this moment and this heavenly feeling. Nothing before mattered, and nothing afterward counted as much as now.

She thought her heart would burst from the longing and desire bottled up in her for so many years.

Then Carl slipped Sandy's dress down her arm, and suddenly she realized what was happening. She felt surely she would explode into a million little pieces of anxiety. Carl wanted more from her than just a kiss!

Suddenly it all came back, the reason for her reserve, the vow she had made. Men were not to be trusted, even one as magnetic and persuasive as Carl Van Helmut. He obviously had planned this little encounter. It had not happened by accident.

While she couldn't deny she still harbored normal feelings of sexual desire, she could and would deny their expression. She would never fall into the trap of giving herself to a man again.

Suddenly, she pulled free of Carl's embrace. Her eyes blazed with anger.

"Just what do you think you're doing?" she asked, pulling her dress strap back onto her shoulder, her hand shaking.

"Only what we've both wanted," Carl replied. His eyes narrowed, piercing into hers as if searching there for confirmation.

"Speak for yourself," Sandy retorted. How dare

he assume he knew her so intimately as to know what she wanted?

"Sandy, I merely kissed you. That's hardly a federal offense. I enjoyed it, and you did, too. What's wrong with a man and a woman enjoying each other?"

"You wouldn't understand," she mumbled. For the first time in years, tears threatened to spill over, but she fought to keep her eyes dry.

She pulled her lips taut to still a quiver. She sucked in her breath and drew her shoulders up arrogantly.

"I'll thank you to keep our relationship strictly business," she said, hoping he didn't hear the quaver in her voice.

With that she turned on her heel and marched away.

No matter how attractive she found Carl Van Helmut, she didn't want him to kiss her . . . now or ever!

Chapter Five

*S*andy lay in her darkened apartment, a street light slicing through the break in the drapery by her bed. Tears trickled down her cheeks.

She thought she had buried forever the memories that had haunted her and sent her fleeing for the safety and anonimity of the big city. For years she had refused to allow the old agony to rise to the surface of her imagination. But something about Carl Van Helmut had rekindled the spark, and a fire of raw pain licked at her emotions.

She had been so young then, and innocent. The small Ohio farm where she grew up had not prepared her for the hard cruelties of life. Her father had been what they called a part-time farmer. He worked in town during the week at the local grocery store and farmed the fifty acres they leased on the weekends. Her mother canned the vegetables from their garden, sewed all her clothes and took care of the farm animals during the week.

It was a quiet, uneventful life. Mildred Carver, Sandy's mother, was a warm, loving woman. But her father was a quiet, distant man. While Sandy knew he loved her, he was not demonstrative.

Sandy plucked chickens, rode horses and spent a lot of time outdoors. After high school, she scraped together enough money for a year of college, but she had no idea what she wanted to study.

It was a shock when her father died suddenly. She had never faced a major trauma in her life. At first she found herself in a state of bewilderment, not quite knowing what to do.

People from the church dropped by, brought food and offered their condolences. The funeral was drab. Then Sandy and her mother were left alone to cope as best they could with their grief.

Her mother needed her. So she didn't mention returning to college. She located a job in a fast-food chain, dispensing ready-made burgers and hating it. It was a dead-end job, and she wondered if she would spend the rest of her life there.

One evening, a slender, tall customer entered the diner. He had long, graceful fingers, a head of curly dark hair and sparkling green eyes. He was in his late twenties and seemed out of place among the teenagers that crowded in after the football game.

"Hi," he said, flashing white teeth as he placed his order.

Sandy smiled. "Hi, yourself," she grinned back.

Green eyes settled on her face. She blushed. She reached up to adjust the pert cap she wore on her long blond hair.

"Anything else?" she asked.

"Not this time," he said and winked. "But I'll be back."

And back he came. The next night, he strode in again, looking over the cash registers. As soon as he spotted the one Sandy operated, he walked over to her.

"May I help you?" she asked.

"You sure may," he said warmly. "One burger, fries, a coke and you."

"What?" she gasped.

"Don't get me wrong," he said. "I'm an artist. You have a lovely face. I'd like to paint you."

Sandy eyed him suspiciously.

"It's no line," he said. "Really. I'll bring some of my work and show you if you don't believe me."

He sounded so sincere.

"Wh-what kind of paintings do you do?" she asked.

"Just about everything," he said. "But I specialize in portraits, especially of beautiful faces."

Sandy dropped her eyes. She had never considered herself beautiful. But it was nice to think someone else saw her so.

"What's your name?" he asked.

"Sandy."

"Mine's Roland Peters." He extended his hand over the counter.

She hesitated and then understood he wanted to shake hands. She placed her hand in his. It was warm, intimate and soft.

Roland dropped in at the burger stand every night for the following week, ordered some food, spoke to her and eyed her for a while before leaving.

She had to admit she was flattered by his attentions. She had dated only high-school boys and one fellow in college. She was between boyfriends, and having someone older and worldly interested in her, even if only to paint her portrait, sent shivers of excitement rippling through her.

One night, when Roland placed his order, Sandy asked, "How long are you going to keep coming in here?"

"Until you agree to sit for me," he said, his green eyes glittering.

"What if I never do?" she suggested.

"Then I guess I'm going to get awfully tired of hamburgers."

They smiled in unison, and Sandy knew she could resist no longer.

"If you'll come home and meet my mother, I guess it will be all right," Sandy said slowly.

"Of course," Roland said. "I wouldn't have it any other way."

He must be on the level, Sandy thought happily, if he was willing to meet her mother.

Mrs. Carver liked Roland immediately. He had a certain charm about him, a cosmopolitan yet earthy quality. He seemed right at home in their large, old-fashioned living room with its worn furniture.

Roland came to her house to paint her portrait, and he fell into staying and eating with them after his work for the day was finished.

One day he came bounding in the front door with an arm load of groceries.

"What's this?" Mrs. Carver asked.

"Food!" Roland exclaimed jubilantly. "I just sold a painting. I've been eating off you long enough. It's time I furnished a little sustenance around here for the family."

Family. Roland had referred to them as a family. Sandy's heart warmed. A lump lodged in her throat.

"You know the fortunes of an artist," he went on, as he set the sack on the kitchen table and began lifting out its contents. "They rise and fall like the tides. It's feast or famine."

"Doesn't that worry you?" Mildred Carver asked, taking a can of soup from Roland's hands.

"I'm used to it," he said nonchalantly.

When the portrait was completed, Roland offered it to Sandy as a gift.

"This is one I'd never sell," he said softly.

Mrs. Carver hung it in the living room, proud to have a genuine oil painting hanging in her home.

And then they had fallen into dating. It seemed the most natural thing in the world.

Sandy loved Roland's "garret," as he called it. It was a small A-frame house he had rented for almost nothing because of its deteriorating condition. But it had charm. The lower floor was paneled with a rich, dark wood, had hardwood floors and a large window looking out on a grove of trees. There was a small kitchen with a beat-up stove and a creaky refrigerator. Roland kept only one place setting of silverware and a cup, saucer, plate and bowl.

"No need complicating life," he explained.

The bedroom was a loft situated at the top of a narrow staircase with a high rail around three sides. Roland had stacks of books in a floor-to-ceiling bookcase stretching along one wall. Names like Spinoza, Kant, Schopenhauer, Santayana, Camus, Jung, Freud, Adler and James filled one entire shelf.

It wasn't long until she and Roland were married. Their wedding gift was the portrait her mother had so lovingly hung in the living room.

Sandy brought a few dishes, pots and pans with her and set up a simple mode of housekeeping with Roland. She quit her job when he insisted his artistic nature needed her for inspiration at home.

At first, Sandy was deliriously happy. Roland was tender and gentle in bed. Sandy had no inhibitions about sex, having been taught it was a natural and beautiful part of life. Their intimacy seemed to enhance their easy, seemingly natural relationship.

Their first year of marriage rolled by in a hurry. Sandy's only concern was that Roland had an inflexible habit of drinking continuously from after supper until bedtime. He often staggered to bed, threw a heavy arm over and snored away the night. But the next morning he was clear-headed and attentive. Since he preferred their romantic encounters in the morning anyway, his drinking didn't interfere with their love life.

And so her life had gone for a time. But little by little, Roland's drinking became worse. And as his drinking became worse, so did his temper.

It was only later that Sandy realized how naive she had been. She had known nothing about the darker side of human nature, about the frustration born of creative impotence, which her husband was experiencing.

Roland began to abuse her, verbally at first. She was frightened. She didn't understand what was happening to their marriage. She blamed herself, trying desperately to find some way to make him happy, to encourage him in his work, to keep things running smoothly around the house.

The more submissive and agreeable she became, the more he took out his anger and frustration on her. It was only later that she realized Roland couldn't compete. When his paintings failed to sell, when he couldn't produce, he took out his frustrations on her.

She didn't know what to do, how to cope with behavior she had never before encountered. She felt ashamed. A despair clouded her thinking, and she stayed with Roland, enduring the physical abuse, certain that time and prayer would change him.

When the abuse became more intense, Sandy developed a frantic search for a solution. None came to mind, but she thought fate had intervened. She had become pregnant. Perhaps a baby was the perfect answer. A child would make Roland see his responsiblity. He would have to grow up. He would have to think about someone besides himself.

Now a sharp pain shot through Sandy's head.

She couldn't think about the past. It was simply too painful. And what was the point? She had rehashed it millions of times, relived the agony over and over again, until she had finally buried those memories where they belonged, in the deepest recesses of her mind.

She had made up her mind that men were not to be trusted. Until now, it had been easy to live with that philosophy. She hadn't met a man interesting or vital enough to challenge her theory. She hadn't met a man appealing enough to make her call out those old ideas and reexamine them.

So why was she torturing herself with the past now? Could it be because of Carl Van Helmut?

No, she refused to believe she could be attracted to a man who rubbed her the wrong way every time they met. Yet she couldn't deny he had some sort of impact on her, some special influence on her reactions.

She had kept her emotions under such tight control that she had never wavered in her belief that there was no place for a man in her life. Was she wavering now?

No, she told herself emphatically. It was only natural for the past to rise up to haunt her from time to time. It would probably happen periodically throughout her life. Carl Van Helmut had absolutely nothing to do with it!

Chapter Six

$\mathscr{I}$ took the dress back to the right department, but nobody was there, so I left it in the dressing room," Gloria pouted.

"Well, it's disappeared, Gloria," Sandy said as gently as she could. "I know it seems like a tough policy, but the model is always responsible for everything she wears. If we can't locate the dress . . ."

"You expect me to pay for it?" Gloria asked. It was obvious she was on the verge of anger. Her blue eyes were watery. Her voice shook.

Maybe she'd better mollify Gloria, Sandy thought to herself. This was one of her better models. Perhaps the dress would be found. There were always problems getting all the merchandise back to the right departments. No matter how careful she was, something was bound to go wrong. Murphy's Law never failed to operate.

"Let's give the girls in the department some time to inventory the fashion-show garments before we get all upset over it, OK? It's bound to turn up. I'll call you tomorrow and let you know."

Gloria grimaced but nodded. "OK. But I sure don't expect to have to pay for something I returned."

"I'll call you," Sandy repeated, walking with Gloria a few steps to usher her out of the department.

Sandy sighed as Gloria left. Then her thoughts turned to the topic that had plagued her since the previous day. No matter how hard she tried, she couldn't force herself to erase from her mind a picture that troubled her. It replayed again and again, and accompanying it were tumultuous emotions she couldn't begin to understand.

In her mental image she was in Carl Van Helmut's arms. She relived repeatedly the whirlpool of conflicting feelings his nearness had stirred up in her. She wanted to blot out the memory of the evening before, but she couldn't. It was a compulsive pattern of crazy thoughts that kept flashing on and off, tormenting her and distracting her attention from her work.

She returned to her own department to check on how things were running. As she approached a rack of designer jeans on the perimeter of the merchandising area, her heart stopped beating. Across the store, she spied a tall frame topped by a thatch of heavy blond hair. Her throat constricted. Waves of emotions she couldn't define spilled over her, making her hands clammy.

What was happening to her? Was she losing her mind? How could the mere sight of Carl Van Helmut bring on this strange feeling of detachment? It was as if her mind floated out of her body, refusing to allow her feelings to reach it.

Before she could analyze it further, Deanna rushed up to her. "You've got to do something," she said agitatedly.

"What's the matter?" Sandy asked. The expression of anger on Deanna's face spelled trouble.

Sandy was almost glad for any kind of problem that would take her mind off herself.

"It's Vergie," Deanna said. She was fuming. "Ever since she helped you with the style show yesterday, she thinks she's in charge around here. She's been giving me 'what for' all morning. I know my job. She doesn't have to tell me what to do."

"What did she say to you?"

"She told me I was encroaching on Ellen's customer and that I took too long for a coffee break. Ellen can darn well look out for herself around here. I can't steal any customer she's really working with. And I had to go to the ladies' room on my way back from the coffee shop. I was only a couple of minutes overtime. But Vergie made a federal case out of it!"

"I'll talk to Vergie," Sandy said. She hoped her noncommital answer would assuage Deanna's anger. She didn't promise to chastise Vergie, who probably would tell a story closer to the truth than Deanna. But she would speak to the woman to find out what had really transpired.

"Well, I hope so!" Deanna said. "I'm tired of being the scapegoat in this department. If anything goes wrong, I get the blame. I think the others are just jealous because I'm the best salesperson on the floor. I work hard for every penny I earn, and I'm tired of having to pay for it by putting up with insults and snide innuendos."

"I can see you're really upset."

"You're darn right I am!"

"Shhh," Sandy said softly. A woman approached them with a knit top draped over one arm.

"Excuse me," she said. "Do you have this in a larger size?"

Sandy looked in the neck of the top. It was a small. "Are you looking for a medium?"

"Yes. My daughter thinks these tops are some sort of status symbol with this little design on the pocket. She has a red one, but now she insists on a blue one. But I couldn't find a medium."

"I think we may have one in the stockroom," Sandy said. "A new shipment came in this morning. Deanna, will you check, please?"

Deanna nodded and trotted off. This would be her sale. Sandy always gave her customers to one of the girls in her department on a rotating basis to boost their sales. As department head, she earned a flat salary. But her salesgirls could earn a commission if they rang up over a certain dollar amount on the cash register every week.

"That is a lovely knit top," Sandy said. "Does your daughter have a pair of jeans to go with it?" Long ago she had learned to sell up, suggesting additional items to her customers, but never putting pressure on them.

"Yes, she has plenty of jeans. Wears them all the time. I can't get her in a dress, except for church."

"Do you think she'd be interested in a pair of culottes or knickers? They're very hot items right now, and I know how teenagers love to be in style." Sandy led the woman to the pants rack and held up various styles of pants for the woman to examine.

"She might be," the woman said slowly.

"These won't last long," Sandy said. She was very enthusiastic about her new line of pants. They had sold well in stores in the North and were featured in display ads in the newspaper. She knew her merchandise and the competition and how well most items in her department were moving elsewhere.

"How much are they?"

Sandy handed the knickers to the potential customer and quoted a price. It was always a good idea to get the merchandise into the hands of the buyer.

"We buy a limited supply of each style in each size. I've checked with our buyer and found out that only one other store in this area is carrying this line, so your daughter can rest assured she won't meet herself coming down the street several times a day. While she'll be wearing the latest style, she'll have her own design."

There was a certain snob appeal in shopping at a quality department store like Van Helmut's. Customers wanted stylish fashions different from what everyone else was wearing. Unlike the discount stores where fifty identical dresses hung from one rack, Van Helmut's limited the number of copies it sold of any particular style.

Patrons paid for both quality and distinction.

"Can I return them if they don't fit?" the woman asked.

"Certainly," Sandy replied, smiling. "Customer satisfaction is always guaranteed at Van Helmut's. Just keep your sales slip."

The woman nodded.

Deanna approached with a blue knit top draped over her arm. "They came in," she said.

"Good. Now, Deanna, will you please see that Mrs. . . . ?"

". . . Cunningham," the woman responded.

"Will you see that Mrs. Cunningham is properly taken care of?"

"Of course," Deanna said. She obviously had calmed down considerably while in the stockroom. Her frown was gone and her voice sounded brighter.

"Why don't you show Mrs. Cunningham the new socks we are featuring to go with the knickers? And we have some really darling tie belts that set off the outfit beautifully."

Deanna nodded.

"Deanna will give you her personal attention, Mrs. Cunningham, to see you find everything you need. I'll be here if you need me for anything, all right?"

"Yes, thank you," the woman said.

Deanna ushered her to the sock display.

Sandy stood watching them for a few minutes, satisfied that Deanna would sell Mrs. Cunningham several additional items. Then she headed for the dressing rooms looking for Vergie.

As she rounded the corner, Vergie emerged from one of the louvered doors behind which stood a customer. Sandy motioned to Vergie with her index finger. "I need to talk to you," she whispered. "See me as soon as possible."

Vergie nodded and whisked past her. Moments later, she rushed back into the hallway with a couple of pairs of shorts over her arm. She gave them to the teen-age customer and took back the ones the girl discarded.

"Where's Ellen?" Sandy asked.

"On her coffee break," Vergie answered.

"I need to talk to her. Think you can handle things for a while?"

"Sure," Vergie said, "if you don't mind a cat fight. Deanna had a fit this morning because I tried to 'handle things.' I know she's a good salesgirl, but she's a real pain in the you-know-what!"

"I know," Sandy said. She was sympathetic to Vergie's complaint. More than once she had been tempted to fire Deanna. Now that she had that power, she felt she could use it to exercise more control over her troublesome salesgirl. It was always better to work with an existing employee and try to upgrade her than to start over with a new recruit who was an unknown quantity. But if it came down to it, she would fire Deanna rather than have the girl undermine the morale of the entire department.

"Can you try to smooth things over until I can get to the bottom of the problem? I'm counting on you."

Vergie smiled. "Sure," she said. "I won't blow my stack."

Sandy returned her smile and headed for the coffee shop. Seated at the various tables were several employees. Julia French walked in behind Sandy.

"Hi," Julia said. "Want to join me?"

"Yeah, in just a minute. I have to speak with someone first."

Julia nodded and got in line at the counter. "I'll get you a cup of coffee."

"Good. Appreciate it." Sandy waved her hand in thanks and looked around for Ellen. The girl was seated in the corner by herself.

Sandy strode briskly over to her. "Hi," she said. "Mind if I sit down a minute?"

Ellen looked up. "Of course not," she said. She motioned to the chair next to her. But the expression on her face said she knew this was more than a social gesture.

"Anything wrong?" Ellen asked, her voice registering higher than normal.

"Not really." Sandy pulled the chair out and sat down. "It's just that Gloria Richards, one of the models in the fashion show, seems to have misplaced an expensive dress from the junior department. She says she left it in the dressing room this morning. Did you see it? It was red denim with white piping around the neck."

Ellen frowned. "I remember the dress. I was there when you picked it out for the show. But I haven't seen it today. What happens if it's not found?"

"I'm afraid Gloria will have to pay for it."

"You don't think she stole it, do you, and is lying?"

It wasn't the kind of question Sandy liked to answer. She preferred to give Gloria the benefit of the doubt. But some models had sticky fingers, just like some members of any other group. Other models were scrupulously honest. Perhaps Gloria had taken the dress, hoping she wouldn't really be made to pay for it. Sandy didn't like being made a fool of, so she wasn't about to deny the possibility of Gloria's dishonesty. But neither could she openly accuse her.

"That's really not the question," Sandy said. It was best to evade the issue. "Our job is to try to find it. When you get back to the department, will you check all the dressing rooms? If it's not there, look in the stockroom. You might even check the racks to see if a customer put it back on display."

"Yes, ma'am," Ellen replied.

Sandy chuckled. Even after all this time, she had not grown accustomed to the southern custom of referring to one's female superior as "ma'am." It happened only often enough to capture her attention, but not frequently enough for her to get used to it.

"How are you and Deanna getting along?" Sandy asked.

Ellen looked down at her paper cup. "Okay." Her voice was weak, unconvincing.

"What's the problem? You can tell me."

"Nothing . . . really."

It was obvious Ellen was scared of Deanna for some reason. The girl probably thought her job was in jeopardy. Deanna had been in the department longer. If there was any dissension, Ellen most likely concluded that she would be the one who would be fired.

"I hope we can get it worked out," Sandy said. She wanted to reassure Ellen. "You're a good worker with a lot of potential. I'd hate to lose you."

Ellen looked up, her eyes sparkling. "Really?"

"Of course. Besides," Sandy laughed, "you still owe me some money. I can't have you leaving until you've paid in full."

Ellen caught the joke and smiled.

"Thanks," she said. "I needed that. I've been a little down lately."

"We all get that way sometimes," Sandy said.

"You never seem to."

"Listen, beneath this glittering exterior there beats the heart of a real pessimist. Only the challenge of running my department keeps a smile on my face. It's never easy, but I love the excitement."

Ellen grinned.

Sandy winked at her and rose. It was odd how she could be so many different people. With Ellen, it was easy to be kind and to tease. With Julia, she could relax and reveal many of her inner feelings. Deanna brought out the rough, hard side of her nature. Sandy sometimes wondered whether she really knew just who she was. Was she the light-hearted department head, as Ellen saw her? Or was she the relentless career woman that Deanna was trying so desperately, but crudely, to imitate? Perhaps if life hadn't shoved her into a box and forced her life-style on her, she would have had the opportunity to find out what she really wanted out of living.

Sandy brushed aside her introspective ruminations. She had no time for such thoughts now.

She joined Julia at another table and took her cup of coffee in her hands. She took a big swig, the hot liquid stinging as it ran down her throat. The pain felt strangely soothing. She was in the mood for a little self-flagellating.

"How's everything going?" Julia asked, obviously aware of Sandy's tension. Her eyes followed the cup as Sandy set it back in its saucer.

"It's the usual madhouse," Sandy laughed wryly. "I guess I'd get bored if things ever settled down to normal. How about you?"

"Same here," Julia said. Her porcelain face reflected a degree of weariness. "But all the headaches don't stimulate me the way they do you. They just get me down. I'd love for my department to run like clockwork, but it never does."

"What's the latest?"

"The newspaper is screaming for some photographs for a display ad, but the new merchandise can't be tracked down anywhere, and the manufacturer swears it was shipped on schedule. We're two weeks behind in production on a special-promotion mail-order catalogue for selected clients, and one of our top items has proved to be a real dog. We're still handling complaints about a sneak preview sale because we ran out of merchandise, and one customer is threatening to turn us over to the Better Business Bureau. As I said, it's just a normal week."

The women laughed in unison.

"It's a good thing we still have our sense of humor," Julia observed, "or we'd both be ready for the funny farm."

"Are you sure this isn't the funny farm?" Sandy asked.

"No, I'm not. But I'm not sure I'm going to hang around long enough to find out. I may just be quitting."

"What?" Sandy exclaimed. The news was totally unexpected.

"It just so happens that yours truly is officially engaged." Julia lifted her left hand from under the table, where she had been holding it in her lap.

A large diamond winked at her.

"Say, that's some rock!" Sandy congratulated her. "And who's the lucky fellow? Brut Van Helmut?"

"Who else?"

"Just checking." Sandy tried to keep the conversation light. She had never told Julia about her past. She had kept that dark secret locked away from everyone. But it simmered under the surface and tainted her enthusiasm about Julia's engagement. The Van Helmut family exhibited a streak of domination that troubled her. "Brut" was such a harsh name. Did he have a personality to match? It was so easy to misjudge a man, to think him kind and caring and wonderful. But beneath that exterior could lurk the heart of a beast.

She'd best keep her reservations to herself, Sandy thought. It was not her business to meddle in Julia's love life.

"When's the wedding?" Sandy asked. She hoped she camouflaged the wariness in her voice.

Julia's eyes sparkled. "We haven't decided just yet, but we're going to set a date soon. Oh, Sandy, he's the most wonderful man. I just know I'm going to be gloriously happy!"

"Sure you will," Sandy said. But underneath, ragged doubts flipped crazily in a storm of apprehension. Carl had already approached her about Julia's character. Would the older brother try to dissuade the younger from marriage with a "commoner"? The Van Helmuts were not exactly the boys next door. They were wealthy, hard-working pioneers who had made something of themselves. Sandy didn't know a lot about their background, but she had a few facts. Would they allow Brut to marry a girl from the advertising department?

"And you're going to quit work when you get married?" Sandy asked.

"We haven't talked about that, yet, but I'd sure like to get out of the rat race," Julia confided.

"If I know the Van Helmuts, they'll probably just give you a promotion and keep you on the payroll. The whole family is involved in some aspect of the business. Mr. Van Helmut's brother runs the branch store and all the wives are bookkeepers or buyers.

Carl Van Helmut was the only maverick until recently, and they even hogtied him into working here, at least in his father's absence."

"It's a real family operation, all right," Julia said. "But I'd like nothing better than to get out."

"Maybe you'll change your mind when you have a vested interest as one of the owners."

"Maybe so," Julia conceded. "But right now, all I can think about is staying home, cooking, cleaning house and having kids. Have you ever wanted children, Sandy?"

The question hit Sandy like an iceberg slicing through her heart. Her muscles went rigid. She clenched her teeth so tightly her jaw ached. A momentary flashback to a tragic scene in the hospital brought a flood of rage surging up in her.

"No," she answered brusquely. She didn't want to shatter Julia's enthusiasm, but it was a subject she couldn't talk about.

"I'd better get back," Sandy said woodenly.

Julia frowned. A puzzled expression skipped across her face.

It was not like Sandy to be so abrupt with Julia. But this was a situation Sandy couldn't cope with intelligently. She could manage her department under the most hectic circumstances; she could stand up to the highest official in the organization and boldly state her case, and she could deal with more than a dozen demanding models and put on a successful style show.

But when anyone approached the inner Sandy Carver, when her emotions about her past were called into play, Sandy knew only one strategy. She ran.

She got up from the table. "Thanks for the coffee," she said perfunctorily.

She strode toward the door, putting as much distance as possible between her and the sound of the words still reverberating in her ears.

Why did these situations always come up when she least expected them?

She could pass by the baby department with her emotions intact because she knew it was there. She had learned to look at newborn infants without flinching. She could read about children in the newspaper and not wallow in the misery of her past.

It had taken time, but she had learned to insulate herself from the pain of her loss. But she had never expected to be asked such a pointed question. She had not been prepared. She had had no time to rehearse the answer in her mind, to fantasize the ordeal over and over again until it lost some of its sting.

An ache the size of a mountain rose within her. Just as she put her hand out to grasp the door handle, it opened, and in walked Carl Van Helmut. He almost ran right into her.

Involuntarily, he protected them both from a collision by grasping Sandy by the hands to stop her.

A knot of fear twisted inside her.

His hands were warm; hers were cold. His hands were large; hers were small. His hands were steady; hers were trembling.

"Glad I caught you," he said, his blue eyes glittering.

She mentally understood the double-entendre, but it failed to reach the portion of her brain where laughter registered.

She looked at him blankly. Waves of panic billowed in her. It was too much, first the memory of the baby and now the reality of Carl Van Helmut. There was only one way to stop the hurt. She would refuse to feel anything.

It wasn't a technique she could always count on. Sometimes it worked. Sometimes it didn't. It might come in snatches. But when she was able to turn off the faucet of her emotions, she could endure almost anything because she detached herself from all sensations.

It was a trick she had learned in the hospital. When life overwhelmed her, she withdrew from the foray.

She took a deep breath and pulled back into herself, deeper and deeper, until she became almost a robot. She heard and felt and experienced, but somehow she cut off the sensations from her brain.

She knew what was happening, and later she could recount the events in detail. But she was like those people who had experienced near death in the books she had read. What happened while they were outside their bodies did not affect them.

"I was just on my way back to the department," Sandy said, pulling her hands back.

"Join me for a few minutes," Carl said.

"Is that an order?" she asked. She smiled politely, but she felt nothing inside.

"Yes," Carl said. He took her elbow. Through the steel wall blocking her feelings, she sensed his touch. How had he penetrated her defenses? She fought harder to blot out the reality.

"Let's sit over here." He indicated a table in the center of the room.

Obediently Sandy sat where he motioned. The

cold plastic chair was hard, but she was unaware of its surface.

"Coffee?" he asked, standing over her.

"No, I just had some."

"Mind if I have a cup?"

"No, go ahead."

He smiled and left her alone for a few minutes. She sat stiffly, trying not to let a picture form in her mind. It was a scene that demanded her attention, but she refused to give it a chance to play itself out.

She would not recall herself in Carl Van Helmut's arms. She would not relive the sensation of her suppressed passion stirred into a smoldering fire, would not reexperience the strangling fear that Carl was not to be trusted.

He returned and sat opposite her.

"I guess you've heard the news," he said. He sipped his coffee while he waited for her answer.

"What news?"

"About Brut and Julia."

"Oh, yes, she just told me. He'll be getting a fine wife. I hope he's good enough for her."

Carl arched an eyebrow.

"I should have expected such a retort from you," he said. His voice was both accusing and amused.

He put down his coffee cup.

Sandy didn't want to look at him. Eye contact was too painful. She would be looking into the eyes of a man who had known her in an intimate moment, a man who had stripped her for an instant of her solid wall of protective reserve, a man who had held her in his arms and kissed her until she almost forgot herself and the danger of letting down her guard.

She stared down at her hands. "Is that what you wanted to talk to me about?"

"Not entirely. You did a fine job on the style show. You exceeded my expectations."

"Thanks," she mumbled.

"Sandy, look at me." The tone was commanding. She lifted her eyes to the level of his throat.

"Sandy, what's wrong?"

"Wrong?" She could manage only an evasive answer.

"I've kissed women before, Sandy, but I never had one react like that. I'm not repulsive. As a matter of fact, most women find me attractive. The Van Helmut name carries a lot of weight. The Van Helmut wealth usually knocks women off their feet. I found you interesting because all of that didn't impress you. I could tell you were not the kind of woman who was looking for status and prestige through a man. I knew you were a little cold, but I figured I could thaw you out. So naturally I was puzzled when you ran away from me. Why, Sandy?"

"Why shouldn't I?" she replied sharply. "I was busy doing my job and you cornered me. Have I once done anything to make you think I welcomed your advances?"

Sandy had raised her voice. Embarrassed, she looked around her. But no one was paying the slightest bit of attention to them. There were only two other people in the coffee shop now, and they were seated near the door, heads bent close together over the table, engaged in an intimate conversation.

"You haven't done anything overt. But there's something electrical between us. Don't tell me you haven't felt it. When our eyes meet, when our hands have touched . . ."

"Mr. Van Helmut, I find this conversation very

embarrassing," Sandy said. Her voice was shaking. How could he discuss what he had done so bluntly?

"Sandy, there's no reason to feel that way. I have to admit you appeal to me. But I can never find out if our relationship can lead to anything while you hide behind that protective shell of yours."

"We don't have a relationship!" she said adamantly. "Except as employer and employee. There is nothing between us except our work." Her voice was shaking now. Confusion ran through her. She wanted to get away, but her legs were too weak to carry her.

"Only because you choose to keep it that way," he said. "I'd like to get to know you better."

"Pick on somebody else. There are plenty of girls in this store who would leap at the opportunity to get to know a Van Helmut on a personal level. I don't happen to be one of them."

"Why not?"

"I can't answer that. Now, is that all? I do need to get back to my department." It was best to keep her tone as impersonal as possible, she thought.

Van Helmut hesitated. A muscle in his jaw throbbed.

"There was one other thing," he said stiffly. "I just thought you might like to know."

She shot him a quizzical look.

"My father's health has deteriorated. Along with the phlebitis he has developed some lung problems. He's turned the store over to me . . . permanently."

Sandy's interest was suddenly piqued. "You're in complete charge now?"

"Yes."

Had he really had full control of the store before,

or had he been under his father's domination all the while since he had returned to the store?

Suddenly, Sandy began to relax. She was treading on familiar territory, her department. She had many ideas for making it the most successful department in the store.

But first she was concerned about Otto Van Helmut.

"How serious is your father's health?" she asked.

"He'll live to a ripe old age if he takes care of himself and follows doctor's orders. It's hard to keep the old man down, but he agreed only after I said I'd stay on permanently."

Sandy wanted to ask Carl his feelings about running the store. She had heard rumors that the two didn't get along at all. Everyone had been surprised that Carl would put foot inside the store, much less take over. Was he so devoted to his father that he'd take on the store for the older man's sake? Or could he only function in the absence of the older Van Helmut?

"Then he's not in any imminent danger?"

"Only the danger that my mother will kill him with kindness." Carl chuckled.

Sandy couldn't help smiling.

"I'm glad to hear it," she said. "And now that you're in charge, I'd like to talk to you soon about some new ideas for my department."

"That won't be necessary," Carl said.

"What do you mean?"

"Forget any changes. Just keep on with what you've been doing."

"But, Mr. Van Helmut," she protested, "we're not selling as much merchandise as I know we can. I respect your father, but, to put it bluntly, he was a fuddy-duddy. There's a new feeling of freedom I want to reflect in our displays. I don't mean anything garish or in bad taste. But it certainly wouldn't cause the roof to fall in if we put a bikini on a mannequin. Girls do wear them, you know. Your father knew it, but he didn't want to admit it."

"My father's policies still stand," Carl said. His tone was clear and decisive. It said there was no appealing his decision. His jaw was set firmly in a stubborn expression.

Sandy wanted to accuse him of turning her down because she had turned down his romantic advances. But to do so would have brought up a topic she couldn't cope with emotionally. Better to keep her conclusions to herself.

"Yes, sir," she said icily. "May I go now?"

He nodded mutely.

Sandy hurried from the coffee shop. She sought refuge in the ladies' room, where hands trembling from a combination of anger and frustration adjusted her lipstick.

It was clear Carl Van Helmut was a hard, determined man. He would stop at nothing to get what he wanted.

If he knew the real Sandy Carver, he wouldn't be the slightest bit interested in her. What attracted him was the plastic girl on the outside, the career girl who knew how to get things done. He saw her as self-sufficient, decisive and capable. Little did he know she was a frightened rabbit hiding in a deep hole of fear.

How was she going to get him to leave her alone? It was her very defense against men whom she found attractive. It was not a trait she could throw off just to get him disinterested in her. It was not a pose. It was a real emotion, integrated into her personality for the past several years, and it had become an innate part of her by now.

Sandy sensed an underlying determination in Carl Van Helmut that frightened her. How could she convince him that she had no room for men in her life? Would she have to run away again?

Chapter Seven

She had had to do it. It hurt, and she wasn't sure it was even fair. But regulations were regulations. Gloria's dress was nowhere to be found; a search of the stockroom, the dressing rooms and the racks produced nothing.

It had been difficult to insist that Gloria pay for a dress she claimed she returned. Maybe the girl was telling the truth. But she had been careless about leaving the dress without making sure somebody knew she had returned it. That was the angle Sandy used in explaining her decision.

"No one thinks for a minute you took the dress," Sandy had said as gently as she could. "But it has to be accounted for. You were the last one responsible for it."

Gloria seemed irate, but she marched to the credit department, through which all clothes were charged to the models, and made good her obligation.

"I wish there were some way to avoid situations like that," Sandy said to Julia as the two of them headed for a sales meeting.

"No matter how careful you are about the rules, somebody invariably breaks them and then wants special consideration," Julia replied. "I wouldn't have accepted the job of fashion-show coordinator for anything."

"Actually, it was kind of fun," Sandy said. It had been a challenge to prove to herself that she could handle it. "But I wouldn't want to put on another one any time soon."

"From everything I hear, you did a marvelous job."

"It was a good job, but not quite marvelous," Sandy said, smiling. She knew her capabilities, but she also recognized her limits.

As they approached the door of the store auditorium, Sandy stiffened. Carl Van Helmut would be speaking to them, and she still recoiled from the memory of his touch. It had been a week since their conversation in the coffee shop. She had not seen him since. His absence had allowed her to breathe easier, but the prospect of seeing him in the flesh again unnerved her.

It was embarrassing to be in the same room with a man who had tried to kiss her and then had spoken to her about her response to him. She was not accustomed to such intimate discussion, to such frankness. She kept her feelings under tight guard, parceling them out in small quantities, but never speaking openly of them.

Sales personnel trickled into the room a few at a time. Julia and Sandy took seats in about the middle of the room. They smiled and nodded to some of the others, carrying on little trails of conversations with first one and then another.

"Did you hear what I heard?" asked the head of the men's department.

"What's that?" Julia asked.

"I have it on good authority that the Van Helmuts are selling out. Do you think any of us will lose our jobs? You know the old saying, 'A new broom sweeps clean.' "

"Whoever told you got things a little mixed up," Julia confided. "We'll hear an announcement this morning that will clear things up."

Julia winked at Sandy. They both knew the many rumors flying around the store. They were based on Carl's takeover. While the news had trickled down through several channels, there had been no formal announcement. Naturally, the information became distorted as it passed from person to person.

However, Julia had learned the news from Brut, and Sandy had heard it directly from Carl. They had already discussed it between themselves but had said nothing to anyone else.

"Congratulations, Julia," said Amy Peterson from the infants' department. "I heard the good news about you and Brut Van Helmut. I can hardly believe it! You must be ecstatic. He's a wonderful catch."

"Thanks," Julia said wryly. "I like to think of him as more than a good catch."

"Oh, well, of course," she said without a bit of sincerity in her voice. "You're going to have it made," she went on. "All that money. You'll never have to work again. I should be so lucky."

Julia smiled weakly.

Amy picked up Julia's hand, eyed the diamond on her ring finger with a wowed expression and let out a low whistle.

"I'm green with envy!" she said.

"There is more to it than just a ring," Julia said. "There's a very fine guy that goes along with this."

"If he's got any more brothers, send one my way," Amy said, rolling her eyes.

Sandy sat woodenly in her chair. How could Amy be so flippant about a serious venture like marriage, she wondered. She obviously had no idea what was involved. There were dangers no one could really warn another about. There were so many unknowns when two people pledged their lives to each other. It was not all fun and games for many people.

"How about Carl Van Helmut?" Julia suggested. "He's single."

A little explosion ripped through Sandy at the mention of Carl's name. She shifted in her chair nervously. She had to change the subject.

"Amy, have you noticed any change in sales in your department?" Sandy asked.

Amy shifted from playful to thoughtful. "No, not really, why?"

"I've noticed a trend lately," Sandy went on. "We have a lot of people from the North flowing in here, looking for warmer weather. Their buying tastes are a little different from ours. I think we're going to have to stock some clothes that look warmer while actually being lightweight. They're so used to dressing for the cold climate it's hard for them to believe we don't need to bundle up like they do in the winter."

"As a matter of fact, I *have* had several requests

for items we don't carry that are sold up north," Amy replied.

"Maybe someone should bring it up at the meeting today," Sandy said. "We have to be aware of the shifting population. You recall when we had a wave of refugees how we catered to them and boosted sales."

"Good point," Amy said. "Well, see you. I'm going to sit with the girls from my department."

Sandy smiled and nodded. She had succeeded in changing the subject and had gotten rid of Amy. She knew how ambitious the girl was. She'd bring up the topic of the Northerners streaming into Texas and take credit for the suggestion to stock merchandise to appeal to them. But Sandy didn't care. Right now, she was too uncomfortable to worry about anything except getting through this sales meeting.

A door at the back of the room opened, and in came Carl with a small knot of men and one woman. They put briefcases on the floor and shuffled papers laid on the table.

Sandy sat rigid. Would it be this way every time she was in the presence of Carl Van Helmut? Perhaps if he left her alone from now on, she'd eventually adjust to being in the same room with him. But somewhere in the back of her mind, she knew her reprieve from his advances this past week was temporary.

Carl stood at the front of the room behind the long table. He wore a dark business suit with a colorful tie. The deep blue material contrasted starkly with his shock of blond hair. There was no getting around it. No matter how she felt about the man personally, she had to admit he was good-looking. But that was all she would admit.

The ripples of conversation subsided as Carl cleared his throat to call the meeting to order.

"It has come to my attention," he said, "that there have been numerous rumors about the Van Helmut department store changing hands. These rumors are due, no doubt, to the fact that my father has retired from the business. Let me assure you that the store is and will continue to be run by the Van Helmut family. Policy will remain the same.

"I am taking over for my father. From now on, this main store will be under my control. Van Helmut's will continue to emphasize quality merchandise at reasonable prices."

Sandy and Julia nodded at each other and smiled.

The rest of the sales meeting proceeded as usual, except for one thing. Sandy experienced a continuing sense of agitation in Carl's presence. She found it difficult to look him directly in the face, even though he apparently was no more aware of her than he was of anyone else in the room.

When the meeting was over, Sandy sighed. Employees stood up around the room, tossing bits of conversation across the room at each other.

Sandy and Julia rose. Sandy tried not to look in Carl's direction, but her traitorous eyes rebelled at her command.

Several people drifted toward the exit. One woman glanced at her watch. "It's time I was getting to my department," she said.

But none of the activities around her registered in Sandy's mind. Her thoughts were trapped in the rooms of her past, while her feelings were slaves of the present.

Twin emotions fought inside her. One was her

fear, and the other was her attraction to Carl. She wanted to deny that he appealed to her. But to do so would be a lie. OK, so she felt something special for him. She could admit it.

But there was nothing that said she had to do anything about that feeling. To let a man get close to her again, either physically or emotionally, was like playing with fire. It was a dangerous game, and one she wanted no part of.

She had never dreamed that rejecting a man could be so painful. The hurt with Roland had been because of the beast that dwelled within him. But the hurt with Carl was from the frightened animal that cowered within her.

"We've set the date," Julia said, breaking into Sandy's reverie.

"What?" she asked absently.

"The wedding date. Brut and I have set it."

"Congratulations. When is it to be?"

"This summer. June fifteenth. And I want you to be my bridesmaid. Carl is to be the best man."

Sandy gasped. "Bridesmaid?"

"Well, certainly. Who else?" Her tone said it was a foregone conclusion that Sandy would accept.

Sandy cringed. Conflicting emotions hammered inside her. Julia was her best friend. She wanted nothing more than to participate in this most special of events in her friend's life. But how could she possibly be in the same wedding party as Carl Van Helmut? It might not make any sense, but the thought of standing up with Julia, flanked by Carl, was more than she could bear.

But how could she explain her fear to Julia? She had never told her friend about Roland. She had learned to pretend that part of her life never existed. It was a dark secret she had hidden from the world. But she had never been able to hide it from herself.

Time had eased the pain, but it had not erased the scars. The emotional damage was permanent.

"Uh, well, I don't know, Julia." It hurt for her to say those words.

Julia's blue eyes clouded. "What's wrong, Sandy?"

"It's just me, something that's kind of a quirk of mine. I—I'd love to be in your wedding, Julia. But I just can't. Please try to understand. It's something I can't help." There was a pleading quality in her voice.

She knew her feeble explanation didn't make any sense. But it was the best she could manage on the spur of the moment. She hadn't expected Julia to spring such news on her, and she'd had no time to prepare a response.

"Maybe you ought to tell me about it," Julia said softly. "That's what friends are for . . . to share things, both the good and the bad."

"Yeah," Sandy said perfunctorily. She was in no mood to debate the merits of spilling her guts to her friend. She just wanted to dismiss this painful subject as soon as possible.

"Guess we'd better get to work," Sandy said hollowly.

"OK," Julia responded. Her tone indicated her disappointment that Sandy hadn't confided in her.

The next week boiled over with frustration. Sandy had to reprimand Deanna, Vergie phoned in sick and Ellen missed a payment on what she owed Sandy.

Waves of anxiety swept over Sandy. She had bundled her world into a neat little package where events fit smoothly into an ordered plan. But lately the wrapping on the package was becoming tattered with unexpected problems.

Already she had considered the possibility that it was time to run again. Every day that idea grew more attractive.

Then an event triggered a renewed determination in Sandy to dig in her heels and fight back once more.

The buyer in her department quit.

Sandy hungered for the job.

She was the most qualified person to step into the vacant shoes. She knew the junior-sportswear department inside and out.

It would mean continued exposure to Carl Van Helmut if she stayed. But the opportunity was too attractive to pass up. It was a new challenge, and the sweet taste of accomplishment coated her tongue.

At each step of her advancement, Sandy had felt that proving herself on the job would restore her self-confidence, would make her complete once again.

And for a while it had. It had allowed her to pick up the shattered fragments of her spirit, but she was never able to find all the pieces. Fulfillment always lay just beyond her grasp.

She continually grasped for more, hoping someday to latch onto the torch of happiness that would warm her soul forever. She knew a rainbow existed somewhere in this world, and at the end of it lay happiness. But she had yet to find it.

Perhaps being a buyer was what she had been

driving toward all along, she thought. Surely that was the ultimate goal that would make her happy. The job was calling to her. She had to have it.

It was with her emotions caught up in a steel band that she entered Carl Van Helmut's office. He sat behind his desk, signing papers.

When he looked up, electricity shot through her. Fear constricted her throat. But determination pushed her feet one in front of the other until she stood opposite him, in front of his desk.

His blue eyes settled on her waist and slowly traveled the distance up her frame, stopping on her face. He arched a heavy eyebrow. He held a pen in his long fingers. For a moment, he looked like a statue carved in bronze.

Why had she come? No job was worth the pain of being around a man who affected her the way Carl Van Helmut did. Attraction and fear knotted together and made her shake inside.

He smiled softly at first, then wider until the skin around his eyes crinkled.

"Good morning," he said. "I haven't seen much of you lately."

Her cheeks stung with embarrassment. She was remembering the kiss. Was he?

"I've been busy." She was determined to be all business.

"I have, too," he said slowly.

Was that intended as an explanation for his lack of attention to her lately?

Suddenly, she wished she hadn't come. Perhaps she had mistaken his intentions after the style show. Maybe if she kept a low profile, he would forget about her.

Instead, she was reawakening his recollection of

her by making herself visible to him. Was the buyer's job really worth the risk? She stepped back and sat in a chair.

"I'm here about the position of buyer in my department," Sandy said. No need to beat around the bush, she thought. It was better to get right to the point. That seemed more professional.

"What about it?" Carl asked. He stared at her intently.

"I want it."

Carl looked thoughtful a minute. "Do you?" he asked.

"Don't tell me you haven't considered me," Sandy said.

Carl put his pen down and leaned back in his swivel chair. It squeaked.

"What makes you think I'd consider you?" Carl asked.

"Because I'm the most qualified person for the job. I know my department, I'm ambitious, I work hard, I learn fast."

"That's true, but what do you know about buying?"

Inwardly Sandy fumed. What was it with the likes of Carl Van Helmut, anyway? Why did he have to make every meeting with her a battle? Couldn't he simply either offer her the job or tell her he had already picked somebody else? Instead, he was the piper playing a tune, and he expected her to dance for him.

All right, she'd dance, if that's what he wanted.

"I know it involves a lot of paper work. I'm good at that. It requires knowledge of fashions and trends. I read *Women's Wear Daily, Vogue, Harper's,* et cetera, regularly, so I keep up with what's going on.

I'd have to travel, and that appeals to me. I learn fast, so what I don't know, I could pick up. You wouldn't go wrong with me, Mr. Van Helmut. I'd make you a good buyer . . . if you'll give me a chance."

"You have no lack of modesty, do you Sandy?" he said with a wry grin.

"Reticence does not gain one promotions," she answered, hoping she hid the swirling conflicts within her.

Carl turned serious and leaned forward in his chair, resting his forearms on the desk. Thoughtfully, he stroked a pencil with his fingers.

"Sandy, you're all you say you are. Intelligent, quick, aggressive. But you're also hard and impenetrable. A certain degree of toughness is necessary to be a buyer. But something about you troubles me. You're almost too hard, Sandy." He studied her for a moment.

A voice from the past told her to lower her eyes. But a newer voice said to look him square in the face.

"Is your concern personal or professional?" Was she treading on dangerous territory to be so blunt?

"A little of both."

At least he was willing to admit the truth, she thought.

"I think it's only fair you give me a chance," she said. "If I don't live up to your expectations, I'll go back to my old job."

"Are you talking about personal or professional expectations?" Carl asked, his blue eyes gleaming with an implied threat.

Sandy refused to dignify the question with an answer. She shot him a defiant look.

"Well?" she asked after a long silence. "Do I get the job?"

"I'll think about it," Carl replied, his tone all business. "I'll let you know."

"Thank you," she said. She hoped the chill in her voice was not wasted on him.

Sandy stopped at the coffee shop on her way back to her department, but Julia was not there, so Sandy didn't stay.

As she approached her selling area, Vergie signaled to her with a crooked finger. Sandy walked over to her.

"Somebody came here looking for you," Vergie said, frowning.

"Did you find out what she wanted?" Sandy asked.

"It wasn't a woman. It was a man," Vergie said. "There was something about him. I can't put my finger on it exactly . . . but I felt very uncomfortable around him. He seemed so intense."

"Did he leave a name?"

"No, but he said he'd be back."

"What did he look like?" Sandy asked, her curiosity piqued.

"He was kind of tall, with dark curly hair."

"Hmmm," Sandy mused. That was not a very helpful description.

"Anything else?"

"He had green eyes, very dark green eyes. And long slender fingers."

A ripple of fear shot through Sandy. She knew someone who fit that description, someone who had taken her life and mangled it. Could it be? No, she was imagining things.

"And, he asked me a lot of questions about

you . . . where you live, if you were married, things like that."

"What did you tell him?" Sandy asked, her voice hoarse with anxiety.

"Nothing. I said I couldn't give out that kind of information. He got a little mad at first, but he finally left. I told him he could wait around for you if he wanted, but he said he'd be back later. He said he'd known you in Ohio."

A dizzying panic gripped Sandy. Her self-confidence was sucked out of her like an unraveled thread into a vacuum cleaner.

She didn't want to believe it; it was too horrible to be real. But something inside her whispered the truth until the sound became a crescendo of torturing reality.

The man who was looking for her had to be Roland!

Roland! The name brought a flood of pain and a swirling of torturous memories she had not wanted to relive. But she could no longer suppress the recollections of what Roland had done to her and how he had caused her to lose the baby. Bitterness like gall filled her mouth as she recalled the scene in the hospital.

Sandy didn't know what time it was or where she was when she came to. A curious mist filmed over her vision. She knew it was quiet and that someone sat beside her. Then there was a stab of pain in her right arm and blackness.

A voice came floating through the fog. "Sandy, you're going to be all right, honey."

Sandy struggled to open her eyes. Pain radiated through her body, making her wince. Her eyelids fluttered open slowly. A fuzzy face gradually came into focus. It was a face she recognized. She frowned, trying to place this person.

The eyes were filled with tears. The expression was haggard. It was her mother.

"Where's Roland?" Sandy asked, frightened.

"I don't know. But he can't hurt you here." Her mother's voice broke. "You're in the hospital."

"Oh, Sandy, why didn't you tell me?" her mother cried. "This wasn't the first time, was it? I knew something wasn't right between you and Roland. But I thought it was none of my business. I had no idea it was anything like this."

Sandy closed her eyes without answering. Something was wrong. She sensed it. Something more than being beaten up by her husband. She felt shaky.

"The baby?" she asked weakly, fearing she already knew the answer.

Her mother's lips quivered. Her eyes filled with tears and she looked away.

"I didn't even know you were pregnant. The doctor told me," Mrs. Carver said softly. "He thought I knew. Why didn't you tell me?"

Sandy stared blankly at the pale-green ceiling. She wanted to cry, but she couldn't. A chilling numbness spread over her.

She'd lost the baby! An empty void shook inside her, but she steeled herself against feeling any emotion. She was beyond pain. She plastered her feelings behind a brick wall where, she resolved, they would remain forever.

"I'll tell you all about it later," Sandy said hoarsely. "Right now, I just want to be alone. Do you mind?"

"No, I need to get some rest anyway. I'll come

back this afternoon. We'll talk then." Her mother gave her hand a warm squeeze.

After Mrs. Carver left, Sandy lay silently in the bed. She stared straight ahead when the nurses came to check on her and give her medicine. Mechanically, she listened to the doctor explain the miscarriage, caused by the beating Roland had given her.

She shut off all her feelings, and a cold, calculating portion of her mind made all her decisions for her. The doctor told her about a women's shelter for battered wives, and she called and made arrangements to move there as soon as she was released from the hospital.

She told her mother briefly and unemotionally what her life with Roland had been like. Her mother wept; Sandy had no more tears to shed.

At first, Mrs. Carver refused to believe it. But finally she had to accept the truth. All the evidence the police had found in Sandy's house had pointed to what she wanted to deny.

Sandy told the police her story as briefly as possible, but she refused to press charges. She wanted nothing more to do with Roland Peters. Just getting away from him was all she could think about.

Sandy moved into the women's shelter and convinced the officials there that her mother was in danger from Roland, too. So her mother shared her room.

"I'll sell the farm, and we'll move away," Mrs. Carver offered. "It's too much for me, anyway, and I have a good offer on it."

Sandy was in no mood to argue. Life in Ohio had become unbearable. There was a sickness in Roland she hadn't wanted to acknowledge. Her love for him had blinded her to the kind of sick, cruel person he was.

It was frightening to realize she had fallen in love and married a man she really didn't know. She had thought she understood him. They had been so happy at first. What had gone wrong? How could he have grown into such a frightening person?

Sandy lived without hope and without feelings. She was a zombie, performing the rituals of life without actually experiencing them.

Her mother sold the farm, but it was an empty smile that Sandy forced to her lips when she heard the news. Roland was out there waiting for her, and he'd never let her leave him. Wherever she and her mother might go, she'd never live in peace. Every day she'd wake up wondering if that was the day Roland would find her. What would he do to her when he did?

Sandy was filled with despair.

Then one day a policeman came to the women's shelter. He spoke with Sandy in a private room with two chairs and an old wooden table.

"I know this has been a hard time for you," he said, "but I have to ask you a few questions."

"About what?" Sandy said. "I've already said I won't press charges against my . . . husband." The word burned her mouth.

The policeman held up several pieces of jewelry.

"Do you know anything about these?" he asked.

Sandy glanced at them. One she recognized. It was a necklace Roland had brought home to her, one he said was real gold.

"Why?" she asked suspiciously.

"Your husband has been charged in a series of

burglaries. Apparently it's been going on for some time. These are some of the items he's suspected of stealing. We just want verification from you if you recognize any of them."

Sandy felt shocked. So that's where he mysteriously got his money from time to time.

The officer's voice implied guilt. Did he suspect her?

"Roland brought that one home to me one night," she said, pointing to the necklace, "but I never wore it."

"Where is Roland?" Sandy asked nervously.

"In the city jail."

"For how long?" A glimmer of hope sprang up in her.

"For a long time, I'm afraid, unless you want to post bond for him. We've got all the evidence we need to send him up for a long stretch. We just wanted to find out if you were involved, but I don't think there's any question you didn't know what was going on."

Sandy let out a relieved sigh. It was the first emotion she had allowed herself to experience since she woke up in the hospital.

With Roland out of the way, Sandy and her mother laid plans to leave Ohio. Neither of them had anything to hold them there anymore.

The money from the sale of the farm paid the hospital bills and gave them plenty with which to travel as far as they wanted and make a fresh start in life.

They decided on Houston. It was a large city where they would be swallowed up by the masses of people. It was completely different from the farm life they had lived. It was a bustling city filled with cars and people.

Sandy found an apartment in the city, and Mrs. Carver decided after a few months to move to a suburb where she could have a garden and a pet.

Sandy had a string of jobs with fast-food chains until she landed the position at Van Helmut's department store. Mrs. Carver invested the balance of her farm money in savings certificates, lived on the interest and what she could make selling her hand-worked afghans, quilts and other items.

Sandy never dated. She took back her maiden name when she filed for divorce from Roland. But she never lived in peace.

Roland was found guilty and sentenced to ten years in prison. But one day he would get out. Sandy lived in dread that he would come looking for her.

Now her fears had come true. Somehow he had traced her here to Houston. He had found her!

Chapter Eight

Sandy stood wide-eyed and frozen as she prepared to face Roland.

The life drained out of her in a rush, swirling around her feet and disappearing into a bottomless pit of despair.

The door handle in her palm felt like granite. Strength oozed out of her, leaving her weak and shaking.

On the other side of the glass double doors stood Roland! He had come back looking for her. He had found her, and a multitude of black memories had become a blinding reality again.

She could not run. She could not cry out. She could only stand immobile and mute.

"Sandy," he said, coming through the doors.

The softness of his voice did not camouflage what she knew about his true nature.

A shiver ran through her. Her eyes darted around wildly.

"Sandy," he repeated. "Don't run away. Please. I want to talk to you."

"How did you find me?" she choked.

"It wasn't easy," he admitted. "It took a long time. But now that I've found you, I'm not going to let you get away again."

"Let's go where we can talk," he said. He reached for her arm.

She drew back.

"Sandy, please. I have to talk to you. Give me a chance. Things are different now. Let me explain."

Sandy's mind refused to accept the reality of Roland's presence. All her nightmares hammered away at her, making her head throb in pain. This was not happening. Her life was not being turned upside down again.

"We have nothing to say to each other." Her voice came out as a strangled whisper. "Just leave me alone."

"I can't, Sandy."

She stared at him, unbelieving. She prayed she could faint, that the ground would open up and swallow her, anything to end this panic.

"I have to talk to you, Sandy. Now." His steely determination convinced her he wouldn't take no for an answer.

"The coffee shop," she said. The words almost stuck in her throat. She wouldn't have to leave the store with Roland and wouldn't have to be alone with him. They would be in the warm haven of Van Helmut's.

"Lead the way," he said.

She walked beside him, her head bowed, staring at the floor. Bitter memories scrambled for attention in her mind, but she fought to shove them away. She refused to relive the past. It was dead, and part of her had died with it.

In the coffee shop, Sandy motioned silently to a table in the corner. There were several employees chatting in various parts of the room. She chose a spot next to a couple of girls from lingerie.

"Do you want coffee?" Roland asked.

Sandy shook her head.

Roland pulled out a chair for her. She moved away from him and pulled out her own chair, refusing his offer.

Roland smiled wryly. "I guess I can't blame you."

Sandy frowned, avoiding his eyes.

Roland sat opposite her. She stared at the Formica tabletop.

"Sandy, I don't know how to begin. I know what I did was awful. But I was so different then. I've changed, I swear. I've had a lot of time to think over what happened, the way I treated you. I want to make it up to you."

Her eyes darted to his face. It was the first time she had actually looked directly at him.

Roland looked older, heavier. His dark hair still curled, and his green eyes still sparkled. But there was a new dimension about him now, a nebulous quality of maturity, perhaps.

"I don't want anything from you . . . except to be left alone," Sandy whispered.

"Sandy, I don't blame you for running away, for getting a divorce. But I have changed. Can't you believe that?"

"Why should I?" she asked coldly.

"Because I still love you. I've never loved anyone else. Do you know how many nights I lay awake in my lonely cell, regretting how I'd treated you? It was only because I loved you that I survived prison life. Do you know what it's like in the *joint*? It's dehumanizing and brutal. I was beaten up many times. And every time, I paid for my sin against you."

Sandy looked down at her hands, twisted into a knot in her lap.

"You're looking good, Sandy. I like your hair long."

His personal comment sent icy fingers flying up her spine.

"How did you find me?" she demanded.

"It wasn't easy. I started with the people your mother sold the farm to. One person led to another. I was determined to find you. I would have spent the rest of my life looking for you, if necessary."

"Roland, I don't want you in my life," Sandy said bluntly. "I'm happy. If you really care anything about me, you'll quietly disappear and leave me alone." Her voice was shaking.

A troubled frown knitted Roland's brow. "I knew you'd feel that way, Sandy."

Why did he have to keep repeating her name? It hurt to hear it come from his lips.

"But I can't just walk away now that I've found you, Sandy. It's not too late to pick up the pieces and go on. I won't interfere with your job, if you want to keep on working. I just want to be with you the rest of my life. It will be just the two of us, the way it was before."

Two! The number was a rapier slicing into her heart. It was supposed to be three of them. But Roland had killed the baby. She wanted to hurl a bitter accusation at him, to tell him that he was a murderer. But the words would not come.

"It's too late, Roland," Sandy said. Her words were cold, decisive.

There was a long silence. Roland looked down, then his eyes met hers.

"I never did tell you much about my childhood," Roland said. "I didn't talk about it because it was so painful. My father was a lush. The old man beat up on me every time he got drunk. Once, he threatened my mother. I stood between the two of them, shouting he was going to have to hit me first. I really thought he was going to do it. When I started doing the same thing to you that my father had done to me, I hated myself. The more I hated myself, the more I took it out on you. But that's all over now, Sandy. I'll never love anyone else, and I know you loved me once. Give me a second chance. Please." His voice was shaking. His eyes were watery.

There could never be anything between them again. But how could she convince Roland? It tore her heart out to see him so contrite. But he had killed any love for him long ago.

"I—I'll tell you what," she said reluctantly. "If you promise to leave me alone for a month . . . not to come near me, not to call or write or contact me in any way, then I'll talk to you again. You're going to have to prove to me you've learned self-control."

"You won't run away again?" Roland asked.

"I won't run . . . if you leave me alone," she said.

"All right, it's a deal. One month." Roland extended his hand to shake on their bargain, but Sandy just looked at him coldly.

The next week was a nightmare. Sandy lived in a state of nervous tension. Was Roland following her?

Every time someone came up behind her, she jumped. Sleep became elusive. She snapped at Vergie and grumbled at Ellen. She threatened to dismiss Deanna unless she straightened up on the job. She was distant toward Julia, wallowing alone in the misery of her situation.

Then one day Carl approached her on the floor. Sandy stiffened.

"I have good news for you," he said. "The job is yours."

She stared at him blankly. "What?"

"The buyer's job. It's yours."

"Oh," she said vaguely. She had temporarily forgotten all about it.

"I thought you'd be a little more enthusiastic," Carl said. "You did want the job, didn't you?"

"Of course. I've just been a little distracted lately, that's all."

"A problem of some sort?"

"It's nothing," she lied.

"There's a buying trip coming up soon. You'll need to prepare. There's quite a bit of paper work involved, and you need to learn it before we go."

"We?" Sandy asked.

"Yes, I'm going on the trip, also."

A warning bell clanged in Sandy's mind.

"I've decided on a replacement for you," Carl went on, apparently oblivious to her reaction. "I'm promoting Deanna."

"Deanna?" Sandy gasped. She had almost fired her that morning.

"Yes, she has the same kind of drive you do. She's a little rough around the edges, but she learns fast."

Deanna? The same kind of drive? No, she refused to believe she was anything like Deanna. It couldn't be true. He was mistaken. But that was not her problem. He was the boss. He could promote whom he pleased. She wasn't going to enjoy working with Deanna, but she had other more pressing problems to worry about. By comparison, Deanna seemed a mere triviality.

It was a blessing to have forms to pore over and new procedures to learn. It kept Sandy's mind off her inner turmoil, at least part of the time.

The spring buying trip to New York would be for fall and winter merchandise. Sandy had to review the previous year's sales, determine what was new in the market by reading current trade publications and check the most popular price ranges in her department.

Under different circumstances, she would have been excited about her promotion. But a hollow dullness in her heart dampened her enthusiasm, and she completed her chores mechanically.

It was a tremendous relief to fly away from Houston for New York. Even though she sat beside Carl on the flight, Sandy preferred being anywhere except in the same city with Roland.

It was not unusual for the boss to make buying trips, Sandy knew. Otto Van Helmut had often jetted off across the country to supervise seasonal purchases for his store. But Sandy suspected Carl chose to go on this particular trip just to keep an eye on her.

She had been given a staggeringly large budget, and every garment she selected would have to pass the scrutiny of the teen-age buying public. Many misjudgments could cost the department dearly.

The plane carried buyers from every department of the store. They would all stay at the same hotel in

New York, have dinner together and attend several fashion shows while there.

It could have been an exciting trip. Sandy had never been to New York. But a dark stain from her past blotted out much of her enthusiasm.

"I want to give you a few tips before you go to the first showroom," Carl said, breaking the silence.

Sandy looked over at him. He was smiling at her. He looked so clean, handsome and healthy in comparison to Roland. There was none of the dark, brooding quality about him that she had seen in her ex-husband. He was a man with purpose, a man who zeroed in on what he wanted out of life and fought for it.

He was so close to her that her breath became ragged. Their legs almost touched. An intimate warmth radiated from him. She tried to ignore it, but it seeped all around her and enveloped her in a cozy embrace. Chills shot through her.

Why did Carl Van Helmut affect her this way? She could not deny her attraction to him. But neither could she forget the emotional carnage heaped on her by Roland.

Her fear was greater than Carl's appeal. Sandy's thoughts waded through puddles of sadness as she realized how hopeless her future was with any man. She could never overcome her bitter memories. She could never have a normal relationship with any man.

"You're going to have to visit some thirty showrooms, see thousands of garments, select some twenty-five styles from each manufacturer, determine color and sizes for each one, make notes so you can write your orders later and then see to it that all the merchandise is delivered on time."

"All right," she said.

"Let me warn you, Sandy,"—his familiar tone made her heart skip a beat—"the manufacturers are artists when it comes to lying. They'll promise you the moon, but don't believe a word of it."

"What do you mean?" she asked.

"They'll promise to take back all merchandise that doesn't sell. Don't believe it for a minute. They'll guarantee fast delivery. They'll tell you every style in their line will make your season. They'll promise you advertising money to push certain styles and then renege. They'll try to give new buyers a later completion date, the date when they promise to have the merchandise in the store, telling you it's the earliest they ship. They'll try to pass off cheaper merchandise as their top line. You have to be on your toes at all times. Don't take their word for anything. Look at each garment yourself. Check the number of stitches per inch on the seams. Look on the inside; see if the seams are properly bound or pinked. Examine the colors near the window in the daylight to determine if they look different than in the artificial lights of the showroom. Put your hands in the pockets to determine if they're too shallow."

Sandy knitted her brow in a puzzled frown. How did Carl know so much about the business? Rumor had it that he had long ago broken away from his father and the store. Yet he had stepped right into his father's place and had run the store like a pro. Now he was giving Sandy advice only a retailer who knew the business from top to bottom would know.

"I'm impressed by your knowledge of the business," she said. "I'd heard you had nothing to do with the store. But you seem to understand every aspect of it."

"You can't believe rumors," Carl said. "I grew up in this store. My absence the last few years hasn't erased what I learned."

"I'm going to accompany you on the first few trips," Carl said. "I'll show you the ropes, answer your questions, and then you'll be on your own."

He looked at her thoughtfully. Her heart wanted to go pitter-patter. But a chill raced through her and kept her pulse pounding at a steady rate.

"Think you can handle it?" he asked.

"Sure," she said. She hoped the hesitation in her heart didn't come through in her voice. She had practically demanded this job. At the time, she had absolutely no doubts about her ability to handle it. But now, here on the plane next to Carl, hearing his many admonitions and thinking about the incredible amount of money at her disposal, she felt her self-confidence beginning to waver.

"I've got pretty good taste," she added, more to reassure herself than to convince him.

"That's true," he said. "Good taste can be acquired through environment and education. But superb taste is difficult. It's almost an inborn trait, brought to fruition by practice, study and an innate sense of good quality. On this trip you'll find out just how accurate your judgment about quality is. In fact, Sandy, you'll learn a lot about yourself on this trip."

"What do you mean by that?" she asked. His statement had sounded almost like a threat.

"I mean you're going to be pitting all you are against the most skilled merchandisers in the world. You're going to run up against all types of people, many new situations, and you're going to have to make your decisions in a hurry. You'll find out just what you're really made of. Can you really stand the heat in the kitchen? You'll have the answer after this trip."

"You make it sound like some sort of trial by fire," Sandy said. She didn't know whether to feel glum or challenged.

"In a way, it is," Carl said, his eyes glittering as he looked at her. "A trip like this can make or break your confidence. I know you have a pretty good opinion of your abilities. That's why I chose you for this job. Now you're going to get to test those abilities in the big leagues."

Sandy gulped silently. Had she been too eager to move up in her career? Was she really ready for New York? Would she be able to choose the styles that would sell in Houston? She had an incredible amount of money at her disposal.

It was too late to back out now. No matter how inadequate she might feel, she was determined to give this trip her best shot. It might not be good enough, but she'd never know unless she tried, and one thing she was not was a quitter.

The hotel in New York was old but elegant. Sandy was surprised that America's foremost city was so different from what she expected.

Houston was sprawling, modern and mobile. Cars raced over hundreds of miles of freeway, sometimes inching along during rush-hour traffic. Manhattan was compact, older, and most people there depended on public transportation. Sandy felt as if she had stepped into a granite cavern when she set foot on a sidewalk lined with skyscrapers as far as she could see.

Everyone from Van Helmut's department store

stayed on one of two floors in a towering hotel with a view of the East River. Sandy felt a certain sense of security wedged in the middle of the group of buyers from Van Helmut's as they ate supper in the hotel restaurant.

Carl sat opposite her. Every time she looked up, he was staring at her, as if sizing her up. Conversations about the new season took up most of the evening, and Sandy returned to her room exhausted.

She slipped into her nightgown, combed her long blond hair and stared into the mirror above the dresser.

"You may have bitten off more than you can chew," she admonished her reflection.

She was startled by a tap on the door. Gingerly she approached it. "Wh-who is it?" she called out softly.

"Carl Van Helmut," came the masculine voice from the hallway. "Open up."

Relief washed over Sandy. It was someone she knew. She had heard stories about strangers knocking on hotel-room doors in the large city. She retrieved her robe from the closet and slipped it on.

She opened the door. The light from the hallway silhouetted a tall frame topped by a thatch of thick blond hair.

"May I come in?" Carl asked.

"It's kind of late. I'm awfully tired," Sandy protested gently. It made her nervous to be alone with Carl. But she dared not let him know it.

"I just want to give you some last-minute instructions," he said.

"A-all right," she said, standing aside.

He brushed past her. His body warmth swept over

her, making her knees go weak for a moment. A piny aftershave lotion wafted in the air. She tried not to notice its aroma.

Carl motioned for Sandy to take one of the overstuffed chairs in the room. She looked down at her robe. Was she dressed appropriately to have a man in her room? she wondered. She hugged her robe tightly around her, as if wrapping herself in a blanket of safety, and sat down. Her cheeks turned scarlet. She fought to hide her embarrassment, but the more she tried to pretend she was comfortable, the more her cheeks stung with a rush of blood.

Carl sat opposite her. His eyes settled on her face, then trailed down her body. He opened his mouth as if to speak and leaned forward, an intimate expression playing across his face.

Sandy felt her cheeks go pale. Her heart pounded. Was he going to embarrass them both? she wondered, anxiety leaping in her heart.

A deathly silence undergirded the long pause when the two pairs of eyes locked into a visual embrace, one struggling for supremacy, the other begging for anonymity; one probing, the other retreating; one challenging, the other withdrawing.

Sandy looked down at her hands clasped in her lap. She swallowed hard, trying to find her voice.

"You had some instructions?" she asked.

Sandy sensed the disappointment in the air as Carl slowly leaned back in his chair.

"Yes," he said hoarsely. "But I can see you're tired. It can wait until morning."

And then he was gone. Sandy didn't understand the empty feeling that crept into her heart as she crawled wearily into bed.

* * *

The excitement of New York blotted out all of Sandy's doubts about her ability to handle her job.

First, the whole group of buyers from Van Helmut's went to the buying office in the garment district on Seventh Avenue. Carl took Sandy to the cubicle for the junior department, where Sandy got tips on who was showing what and arranged her schedule of visits to showrooms.

The next few days became a blur of elevator rides, visits to large and small showrooms, and style after style from which Sandy would have to choose.

Carl accompanied her the first day to give her pointers on coping with the merchandisers. Sandy was fascinated with the different types of showrooms. Some had bare floors with racks of clothes stuffed into a small area. Others were spacious, boasted carpeting and offered coffee, sandwiches and live models displaying the clothing.

One showroom had a beautiful waterfall in the middle and a spiral staircase, down which floated models adorned in the latest styles. Another showroom was an auditorium with a stage. Buyers were handed a catalogue of styles modeled at a distance. One showroom featured models that would don any style a buyer showed an interest in and would allow the buyer to walk right up to the model and examine the garment on her.

The majority of the showrooms Sandy visited had salesmen who held up the clothes on hangers one at a time, verbally detailing their many selling features.

Sandy kept copious notes, took some samples of materials and began to feel almost dizzy from the fast-paced excursion.

Carl seemed to be taking it all in stride. But it wasn't his neck on the chopping block, Sandy thought wistfully, as she realized the full magnitude of her responsibility.

She, Sandy Carver, was making all the decisions for what would be sold in the junior department the following season. Was it possible to outguess the fickle teen-age public months in advance? A new singer could burst upon the scene and change their dress habits overnight A new fad could sweep the country and send them to the stores clamoring for an item she had not purchased. There was no telling what her clientel would like or hate by the time school started the following September.

Suddenly, Sandy gained a new respect for the difficult job a buyer had. And she wondered if she was worthy of the position. Maybe it had been a mistake to insist on this job. She had been a success as a department head. Would she be a flop as a buyer?

For the next three days Sandy was on her own with the merchandise. She saw Carl and the other buyers intermittently during the day. At night they went out in a group for dinner and a Broadway show.

The excitement of the evening helped her forget her worries during the day. There was a magic about New York, an electric vibration that penetrated the soul and gave one the feeling that something important was about to happen. Sandy sensed the throbbing undercurrent of the city, which came alive at night in a way Houston never had for her.

She enjoyed the brisk walks down the crowded sidewalks as the whole group from Van Helmut's marched en masse from place to place in the evenings. One night, as they passed a park, Sandy and

Carl were at the head of the entourage. Carl nudged her with his elbow and cut his eyes to the left. Sandy looked in the direction he indicated. A big, burly fellow, staggering with the gait of the inebriated, made a crooked path toward a bush near the sidewalk. He stopped at a water fountain, reached into his pocket for a pair of black socks and washed them out in the water. Carefully he squeezed them out and then gingerly arranged them on one of the bushes to dry.

Carl and Sandy chuckled together. It was good to laugh after a hard day's work.

Carl reached over and touched Sandy's hand. She didn't pull back from his touch. The warmth of his hand seeped through to her innermost being and was transported to her heart. He squeezed her hand and she squeezed back gently, shyly.

Carl looked over at her and smiled. She looked down.

The evening was almost at an end. For a reason she didn't understand, Sandy didn't want this moment to pass. Somehow, she had become a part of this great, vibrant city, and her soul ached to hang onto that feeling.

There was silent music in the air; there were invisible birds singing a song only she heard. New York had become a magic carpet transporting her to a world and time beyond herself, to a different sphere of being that was opening up in her new vistas of feeling she had never before experienced. She didn't understand what was happening, but for the moment she didn't care. She just wanted to exist in this realm as long as she could. She felt abandoned, free, unfettered, and it was a glorious sensation.

Sandy was hardly aware of where she was going.

One by one, the others in her group said good night, drifted off to their rooms and were swallowed up by the interior of their hotel.

Sandy found herself at her hotel-room door in the company of Carl. He still held her hand. She looked down at their hands. She wanted to blush, but the blood refused to rush to her cheeks.

She felt detached from the scene, as if she were outside herself watching her alter ego looking up at Carl. She blinked slowly, as if in a trance.

"May I come in?" Carl asked huskily.

Mutely, Sandy nodded.

She handed him her door key. He slipped it in the lock and turned it with a click. He paused, his hand on the knob, staring at her intently. Then he pushed the door open and followed her inside.

She tossed her purse onto the table beside the chair.

Carl came up behind her and put his hands on her shoulders. Strong fingers gripped her flesh. Sandy moaned softly and leaned her head back against his hard chest; her eyes closed.

She was sealed off from the rest of the world. She was no longer Sandy Carver with a past. She was a woman isolated in an instant in time, a woman with deep feelings and passions too long suppressed. She was a woman with a throbbing need unmet for years, and she was alone with the one man who had touched her heart enough to stir in her a longing she had denied she could ever again experience.

She became aware of her entire body, the flesh from the top of her head, down her shoulders, along her arms and out to her fingertips, around her torso, and down her legs to her toes. Every inch of her skin tingled and sprang alive with a throbbing urgency stirred up in her somehow in this city of unrestrained passions.

Sandy grew weak as Carl's warm hands caressed her arms. She leaned her head to one side, and he kissed her on the side of the neck. He nuzzled her with his chin and an explosion ripped through her.

She heard a metallic sound and realized only vaguely that it was the sound of her own dress being unzipped.

The soft fabric stroked her tingling flesh as it slipped to the floor. Carl stepped around in front of her, his eyes melting over the curves of her body.

He clasped her hands in his and slowly drew them to his shirt, directing her fingers to undo the buttons. When her hands remained immobile, he worked them for her. Then he laid the palms of her hands on his bare chest. The mat of thick, curly blond hair felt soft and luxurious.

Slowly, his eyes capturing Sandy's attention with their intensity, Carl shrugged out of his jacket and shirt in one smooth movement. They fell to the floor around his feet.

Sandy looked down at their twin garments, touching each other around their ankles. She should have been concerned, she realized dimly. But she wasn't.

Nimble fingers slid the bra straps from her shoulders. Carl reached around her and unhooked the garment behind her back. His strong arms encircled her momentarily, and her breath came in ragged snatches.

All of a sudden, she felt cool.

Carl's blue eyes wandered slowly over the terrain of her anatomy, obviously admiring the countryside. He smiled. His lower lip quivered.

Then he bent over and touched his warm lips to

her bare flesh. A shiver shot through her. Involuntarily she wrapped her arms around him and pulled him closer, moaning audibly. Her whole body throbbed rhythmically.

Warm hands caressed her flesh. Sandy molded herself in the direction of the movement of Carl's hands over her body. A deep ache welled up in her, sending her senses reeling. She swayed. Strong arms encircled her and bore the weight of her body, which her limp knees could no longer support.

She was carried to the bed and gently laid on its silky cover. The cool fabric sent a shiver racing along her backbone, and she shuddered.

But the warmth of a strong body covering hers chased away her goose bumps, and she relaxed. She became a flowing river, going wherever its banks took it, not caring how fast it coursed, not concerned about its destination.

She was a balloon released into the atmosphere with no will of her own. She was nothing more than a bundle of sensations, without a past or a future. She just was.

"Oh, Sandy," Carl said huskily. "I've waited for this for so long."

The sound of his voice penetrated on her conscious being. Gradually she realized that what was happening was reality. She was not lost in a dream after all.

This was reality, and she, Sandy Carver, was about to let a man she really barely knew make love to her. She was about to toss away the tough lessons life had taught her and give in to the passions of the moment.

Her eyes grew wide as she looked down at her

half-nude body. This was terrible, to forget the lessons of the past.

Even worse, Carl was already half undressed, and he was beginning to remove his trousers.

An electric jolt thrust her mind into the present, and reality captured her in its clenched fist. What was she doing? she asked herself wildly. Hadn't she learned long ago that men were not to be trusted? Hadn't she vowed never to put herself into a man's hands again? Why was her traitorous body clouding her judgment?

She recoiled and slunk back from Carl on the bed. She jerked the bedspread and thrust it in front of her, shivering behind it.

"No," she said flatly. "No. I don't want this. Please go."

Carl shot her an angry look. "What do you think you're doing?" he demanded. "You knew why I came into your room. You let me in. You wanted this as much as I did." His face was red with rage.

Sandy cringed. She had learned long ago that it was impossible to know the true depths of a man until he was forced into a tight corner. Only then would his true character surface.

Suddenly, he came to her. She ducked her head into the covers and froze. She waited for the first blow. . . .

Chapter Nine

Sandy, what's the matter with you?" Carl demanded, his hands gripping her shoulders like a vise.

Tears rolled down her cheeks. She sat huddled under the bedspread. He reached inside her cocoon and lifted her chin with his hand.

"You're crying," he said softly. "You're not just a tease, are you, Sandy? There's something deeply wrong."

She couldn't answer. She choked back the tears. But she refused to look at him.

"Do you want to talk about it?" he asked gently.

Sandy shook her head.

"I wish you would, Sandy," he said, standing up. He zipped his trousers. Then he picked up his jacket and shirt and put them back on.

"There's an attraction between us, Sandy," he went on, sitting on the bed and handing her her clothes.

She sat with her head resting on her knees. A dull ache throbbed inside her.

"But every time we become physically involved, you freeze up. However, each time you've let me go a little further. That wall you hide behind is crumbling. Next time, Sandy, I predict it's going to tumble down completely."

"Next time?" she gasped.

"You know there's going to be a next time, Sandy. We have something that neither of us can deny. I don't know why you won't admit it. I don't understand what demon possesses you. But you almost gave yourself to me willingly. You can't come that close and then back off and pretend it will never happen again. You can't deny you feel something for me, Sandy. It's there, and we both know it. If you can just overcome whatever barrier stands between the two of us, you can relax and enjoy our relationship."

"That will never happen," she said coldly.

"What makes you think not?" Carl asked.

"Because I don't want it to happen," she said. She hoped he caught the haughty tone in her voice.

"One part of you doesn't want it to happen. But a deeper, more compelling part of you can't resist me."

"You're not burdened with modesty, are you?" Sandy asked cryptically.

"I'm just realistic," he said. "I know what I feel for you, and I can sense you return those feelings. You're attracted to me just as much as I am to you. But for some insane reason you don't want to admit it, and you refuse to give in to your deepest longings. But I know human nature. You can deny your basic emotions only so long. In the end, they will win out.

And you'll give yourself to me. Mark my words. You're mine, Sandy. It's just a matter of time until you realize it yourself."

"Don't hold your breath," she said.

Carl smiled. "See you in the morning," he said. He tucked his shirt in his trousers and was gone.

Sandy leaned back limply against the bed pillows. The life had been drained out of her. She felt empty, alone, cold and cheated.

She could never relate to any man again as long as the specter of Roland haunted her. Did she want to spend the rest of her life single? But what could she do about it? Roland had forced himself back into her life, reawakening the old, painful memories.

She doubted she could afford counseling. Besides, there was no guarantee it would work. She felt like damaged goods. She was fatally flawed. There was no cure for what was wrong with her.

Besides, even if she could somehow be magically cured of her emotional trauma, she would never marry Carl. She couldn't trust him any more than she could trust Roland.

Carl had no intention of marrying her. He probably didn't even love her. He was merely attracted to her because she was different from the other women he'd known. He wanted a "relationship" with her, nothing more.

Was she willing to settle for that?

Back in Houston, Sandy buried herself in her work. There was a great deal of paper work to complete in order to finalize her orders. She exhausted herself every night by staying up late and working on her orders. She scrupulously avoided Carl and saw him only occasionally at work.

She drove the girls in her department, demanding that Deanna work overtime. She ignored the grumbles and complaints from Vergie, Ellen and the new girl hired to take the position vacated by Deanna when she was promoted to Sandy's former position.

One day in the coffee shop, Julia stopped by Sandy's table. "Hi, mind if I join you? I haven't seen much of you lately," Julia said.

"Please sit down." Sandy smiled. It was a pleasure to see a familiar face of someone who wasn't out of sorts with her. "I've been staying pretty busy."

"So I hear," Julia replied, setting down her cup of coffee. "You've gotten something of a reputation since moving up to buyer. You must be under a lot of pressure."

"I guess I am, and it shows," she said.

"Do you think you can handle the job?" Julia asked. Her tone indicated she was concerned.

"It's not the job," Sandy said. Her bottom lip quivered. "It's so many other things."

"Hey, you need to talk to somebody," Julia said softly.

"Yes, I guess I do," Sandy admitted weakly. "But we can't talk here."

"Come on, let's both take the rest of the day off," Julia said, taking Sandy by the elbow and helping her to stand. She picked up both paper cups and tossed them in the trash can. "I'm caught up, and you need a break."

Sandy had no will to resist. She felt almost dead inside, but a spark of life remained, and that spark knew its only hope for existence was to expose itself and ask for nourishment.

"Let's go to my apartment," Sandy suggested. "It's quiet there."

"Sure," Julia agreed. "Let me just phone in and let them know I won't be back today." She stopped at a phone in one of the departments, made a brief call and nodded that it was taken care of.

It wasn't long before Julia and Sandy were entering the door of Sandy's apartment. They had climbed the back stairs and entered through the kitchen. It was a modest dwelling, with hardwood floors and area rugs. Through the small dining room off the kitchen, they passed through a large bedroom, through a tiny entryway and into the living room.

Sandy had made bookcases with concrete blocks and wooden boards. Her couch was inexpensive but well cared for, as was the matching chair. She had purposely avoided hanging any paintings on the walls. She wanted nothing in her quarters to remind her of her painful past.

Instead, she had arranged attractive tapestries made by her mother to decorate the walls.

Sandy sank onto the couch. Julia sat at the opposite end.

"Sandy, you look tired," Julia said. "You've been working too hard. Something's bothering you. You haven't seemed quite yourself for a long time. I've wondered what it was, but I felt it wasn't my place to ask. I thought you'd get around to telling me when the time was right."

"Oh, Julia, everything is such a mess. I just don't know what to do about it," Sandy blurted out. "My world is crumbling right before my eyes, and I feel powerless to stop it. I've prided myself on being in control for so long. . . ." Bitter tears stung her eyes.

"Why don't you tell me about it," Julia prompted softly. "I'm a good listener." There was a pause.

"It's not the job, Julia. Oh, sure, I had my doubts when I was in New York. There were so many showrooms and thousands of styles to choose from. It was all pretty bewildering. But I made up my mind I could do as good a job as the next person."

The words tumbled out of Sandy's mouth in a torrent. They had been walled up behind a dam of shame and humiliation, but they could no longer be restrained. They were clamoring to be said, to be loosed so that she could experience some relief from the knot of tension tearing her apart inside.

"Then what is it?" Julia asked.

Sandy's eyes roamed over the furnishings in the room. She needed to visually tack down something real to give her a feeling of stability. She was on the verge of dumping out her deepest secrets on Julia, and the prospect of revealing such a closely guarded part of herself unnerved her.

Not even her mother knew about Roland's return. She had wanted to shield her mother from that development. There was no reason to upset her, when she could do nothing about it.

"I've never told you much about my past," Sandy said slowly.

"I know," Julia said. "I never asked because I didn't want to pry."

"Well, I was married. I grew up on a small farm in Ohio. It was an idyllic, sheltered life. . . ." The painful memories began to crowd in and suffocate Sandy. She paused. There was no point in going into the hideous details of her life with Roland. It was too agonizing to dredge up. "The marriage didn't work out, and I left to come to Houston. Now, my ex-husband is back. He wants a reconciliation."

"After all this time?" Julia asked.

"Yes. He says he's changed."

"That's what has been bothering you?" Julia asked.

"Not entirely," Sandy said. "You see, Carl Van Helmut has taken an interest in me. But I'm not ready for a relationship with a man. . . ." she couldn't go on.

"Are you troubled about having to make a choice?" Julia asked.

"No, I don't want either one of them. I'd just like for both of them to leave me alone."

"Why don't you tell them?"

"My ex-husband is so persistent. And Carl Van Helmut . . . I don't know, Julia. He's an attractive man, but . . ."

"You're confused."

"Yeah," Sandy said, refusing to acknowledge the whole truth to Julia. How could she tell her friend about the cauldron of conflicting emotions Carl had stirred up in her?

"Maybe it would help if I told you something about Carl," Julia said. "I've learned a lot about the entire family from Brut. They're an interesting bunch."

"What good would that do?"

"It might help you sort out your feelings for Carl. He's the reason you declined to be in my wedding, isn't he?"

Sandy nodded.

"He's an admirable man, Sandy. You'd be surprised at the difficulties he's overcome. And I know why he and his father became estranged."

Sandy's curiosity became razor sharp. "You do?"

"Yeah, want to hear the story?"

"Sure," Sandy said, shifting her position on the couch.

"Otto Van Helmut was a hard-working man whose parents came from Holland. He lived through the Depression. Otto's father couldn't speak English. The family migrated to the coastal areas of Texas, where the grandfather began selling odd items from a little pushcart on the street. He distinguished himself by his honesty and hard work, and his little cart grew into a small store, and then into a department store."

"I had heard the family started out with nothing," Sandy commented, "but I didn't know if it was true."

"It was true, all right," Julia said. "It's the typical 'boy makes good' story. Otto Van Helmut was brought up working hard. After school and on weekends, he spent most of his time at the store, cleaning up, rearranging stock, et cetera. The Depression almost wiped out his father's business, and Otto was tempted to take advantage of his customers. But his father reproved him for trying to short-change people. Otto's motives were good. He hated to see his family suffering so. But his father's stern lectures were not lost on him. A rival business failed because of unethical practices, and Otto's father managed to hang on until more prosperous times."

"No wonder he was such a tough old codger," Sandy said with a wry smile. "He'd seen plenty of hard times to toughen him up."

"That's true. But then things got better. The city of Houston grew up around the store, and through the years the store expanded and moved out into the suburbs. But the main store remained in the heart of the city."

"And Otto Van Helmut stayed with the original store."

"Yes," Julia said. "I guess his heart was there. And he hoped his sons would step into his shoes. He brought Carl and Brut up in the same tradition, hard work and honesty. Both boys accepted a lot of responsibility at a young age. They worked in the store and learned the trade. Brut seemed born for this kind of work. But Carl . . ."

"Is this all from Brut's point of view?" Sandy asked, realizing how one brother would color the story of another.

"Not entirely," Julia said. "I've talked at length with Mrs. Van Helmut, and she'd filled me in on a lot of the details. You see, Carl was a sickly child."

"Carl?" Sandy exclaimed, surprised. She could hardly imagine a man as solid, masculine and strong as Carl Van Helmut ever being sick.

"Yes, Carl. He developed asthma as a child. He had frequent attacks. His father had little tolerance for illness. I guess he felt it somehow reflected on his masculinity to have an unhealthy child. He scoffed at Carl's need for rest and tried to force Carl to do more than he was capable of doing. Of course, that created a lot of tension in the home.

"Carl's aunts and uncles tended to coddle him and told him he could never do certain things, such as play sports. While his mother never pressured him, she encouraged him, telling him a person never knew what he could do unless he tried. His father exhibited a great deal of impatience toward him, so they were always in a state of conflict."

"That explains their estrangement," Sandy said thoughtfully.

"In part," Julia agreed. "But there's more. Carl was determined not to let his physical problems hold him back from what he wanted to do. He worked out every day, starting in junior high school, and built up his frail body into a powerhouse. He told his mother he was tired of sitting at home looking out the window at other children playing while he had to hibernate indoors, because physical activity might bring on an attack. At first, the attacks were worse, but he persevered, and gradually his physical health improved along with his strength and stamina. He played football in high school and was captain of the team."

Goose bumps popped out on Sandy. "That's marvelous," she exclaimed. She couldn't help but admire a man who had worked so hard to overcome adversity. It reminded her a little of her own struggles.

"There was another problem. Carl had great difficulty in school. His mother spent hours working with him all through the early years. Again, his father accused him of irresponsibility. He said Carl wasn't trying hard enough.

"Carl was very determined, and eventually he overcame his problems with school. Only later did he learn he had been suffering from a learning disorder called dyslexia. It's a condition which was not even recognized when he was a child. Somehow, the child sees things in reverse. Nelson Rockefeller and some other notables suffered from the same condition and also overcame it. But it takes real determination when you don't even know what's wrong."

"No wonder Carl seems so stern at times," Sandy

said. "I guess with his background, he figures people can do what they want to, if they just work hard enough at it."

"I suppose so," Julia said. "He's certainly made something out of himself in spite of the obstacles life threw in his way. He even bucked his father when he went off to college. Otto thought Carl should go right into the business from high school. Carl knew the store inside and out by that time. But instead, Carl decided to go to college. His mother saw to it that he had the necessary funds. Then after graduation, instead of returning to the fold, Carl began to manage the family's real-estate holdings, learning the investment business, and he built himself quite a nice estate. I think his father held a grudging admiration for his son's abilities, even though he could never quite forgive him for leaving the store."

"I've heard the two have been at each other's throats for years," Sandy observed.

"Yes, they spoke and were civil, but they went their separate ways. Brut thinks Carl couldn't accept a subservient role in the store under his father after he had made himself into a man. It's possible they're too much alike to get along. Brut is a more easygoing type. He's hard-working and industrious, but he's always had a good rapport with his father. Carl was the maverick, determined to make life on his own, not willing to work for anyone else."

"So Carl was able to take over for his father because he knew the business, but he wouldn't have any real involvement with the store so long as his father might return?" Sandy asked.

"That's the story," Julia said. "Mrs. Van Helmut said Otto gave up the business only because he knew it was the only way to get Carl involved. His illness was a blessing in disguise. He could have come back eventually, but he knew doing so would send Carl back to the real-estate business, and he was willing to do almost anything to lure Carl into the store."

"That's very interesting," Sandy commented. "It makes Carl seem so much more human."

"And likable?" Julia suggested.

Sandy stiffened.

"I don't know how serious things are between you two, but I'd like nothing better than having you for a sister-in-law." Julia smiled.

"I'm not interested in marriage," Sandy said. She hoped the brittle tone of her voice didn't sound too harsh.

Sandy couldn't deny her attraction for Carl. He was an admirable man, someone who had faced some of life's most difficult problems and had come out victorious.

How rotten much of his childhood must have been. He'd had to endure the animosity of his father, obviously trying to please the old man, but determined to do it his own way. He was a man with both heart and soul topped with a gutsy determination and steely resolve.

But that was not enough to overcome her own problems with a relationship with a man. Nothing could erase the nightmare she had lived through with Roland. This was not a problem like dyslexia or asthma. This was a problem of the emotions and the psyche. She bore raw scars that refused to heal.

Besides, Carl had never mentioned the word "love." All he felt for her was an attraction. Was that all she felt for him?

How could she know? Roland had intruded on her life once again, and her feelings were a shambles. She felt something for Carl, something she had spent the last several years believing she could never experience again. She hadn't *wanted* to experience it again . . . until she had met Carl. Why had he come into her life and mixed her all up? Why had he stirred in her those passions she had thought dead long ago? How was she to cope with awakened drives that terrified her with their intensity?

She didn't want to feel anything for Carl Van Helmut. So why did her traitorous emotions betray her?

"Do you think you'll go back to your husband? Is there any chance of that?" Julia broke into Sandy's thoughts.

"No!" Was her answer too abrupt? She didn't want to send Julia on a fishing expedition to find out why she felt so strongly. She continued more softly, "It was over long ago. There's nothing left between us. I've tried to tell him, but he insists on seeing me again. He wanted to give me time to reconsider."

"And have you?"

"There's nothing to reconsider, Julia. Believe me when I say it's hopeless."

"I believe you, yet there's something sort of tentative in your attitude toward him. Do you realize that?"

Of course she realized it. But how could she tell Julia it was because she didn't know how she was going to get rid of Roland, that seeing him had brought back all the feelings of hopelessness and despair she'd known during their marriage?

"It's just that he's so persistent," Sandy said. "But

I'll handle it." It had been a catharsis to talk to Julia, but it had been stupid to think her friend could help her solve her problem.

Unless she could convince Roland to stay out of her life, her only recourse would be to run again, which would probably be a temporary reprieve.

The rest of the conversation consisted of chitchat about the store and Julia's upcoming wedding. Now that she understood a little of Sandy's reluctance to be in her wedding, Julia accepted the decision graciously.

The next day, Sandy was called to the phone at work. She placed the instrument to her ear.

"It's been a month," a masculine voice reminded her.

"R-Roland," she choked, her face flaming with bridled emotions. Her hands shook.

"I want to see you. Please. You agreed to meet me. In the coffee shop in ten minutes, Sandy. All right?"

She bit her lip. "Yes—all right." She hung up. Like a zombie, cold and dead, she glanced around the department. "Vergie, will you continue checking in the new arrivals?" she asked, struggling to keep her voice calm. "They're in the stockroom." Sandy was still handling merchandise the previous buyer had selected, and she was becoming more confident, as she recalled her own orders, that she had chosen well.

But right now her job as a buyer plummeted to the bottom of her list of concerns. She wanted to run and hide. But perhaps if she convinced Roland she could never again live as his wife, he might believe she was serious and leave her alone. Surely he would have to see how hopeless his case was.

Rapiers of anxiety sliced through her as she entered the coffee shop. It was almost deserted. A tall, dark-haired figure sat at a table in one corner. Two cups of coffee were on the table. Sandy gulped. Her heart raced as adrenalin surged through her veins. Her deepest instincts screamed, "Run!" But she fought the urge and approached Roland.

He looked at her, his green eyes devouring her. He smiled. "I'm glad you came. Sit down, Sandy."

A pain began in her stomach and radiated out in all directions through her body. She felt both dirty and humiliated. Why was she here? Why did she allow Roland any power over her? Why had she agreed to see him again? She took a seat.

"You're looking good," he said. "But you have circles under your eyes."

"I haven't been sleeping much lately," she said. She hoped he noted the bitterness in her voice.

"I hope that means you've been considering a reconciliation." He stared at her intently.

Defiance bubbled up in her. She narrowed her eyes. "It's because I've been trying to figure out how to get you to leave me alone!"

Shock registered in his eyes. His face paled. Bitterly he said, "You want me out of the way so you can have fun with the boss."

"What are you talking about?" she asked, half angry, half afraid.

"I've heard the rumors," Roland sighed. "And I'll bet they're true. You've become involved with your boss. That's why you want to get rid of me."

Sandy gasped. She was incensed. "What right do you have to go around snooping on me?" she demanded.

"So you don't deny it?" he asked.

"I don't owe you an explanation. And don't think you can scare me," she lied. "I've grown up a lot since you knew me, Roland. I'm no longer the scared kid I was. I want you to get out of my life and leave me alone!"

Suddenly, Roland's expression broke. The tense features melted into painful despair. "I can't, Sandy. As long as there's even the tiniest chance, I can't leave you alone. You're all I've thought about these last eight years. You're all that kept me alive in that hellhole. Don't you understand? I want to make it up to you. I want you to learn to love me again. I'll do anything, Sandy, anything."

The pitiful sight of Roland pleading with her brought back the agony of the night he had beaten her and then begged her forgiveness. He hadn't changed. Not two minutes before, there had been a tone of jealous anger, a threat in his voice. He was the same old Roland, unable to compete, taking out his frustration on others with a combination of whimpering and violence.

A deep shudder passed through Sandy. All of a sudden, she realized with a clarity that she had never recognized before that she had truly been an innocent victim. Somehow she had harbored an ill-defined but strong sense of guilt for years. She had felt that she had been partly responsible for the way Roland had treated her. She had accepted part of the blame, believing that her inadequacy as a wife had contributed to her own punishment.

But now, as she was able to see Roland for the person he really was, she understood how blameless she had been. Her only fault had been in half believing Roland when he'd accused her of being the cause of his failures.

That knowledge freed something in Sandy. And for the first time she was grateful that Roland had come back into her life. For the first time she was seeing the truth. And the picture he presented drew from her a deep feeling of pity. She couldn't really hate him anymore. He, too, was a victim—a victim of the beatings and mistreatment he'd suffered as a child. But though she could find it in her heart to pity him, nothing could entirely erase her fear of him.

"I feel sorry for you, Roland. But I don't love you, and I never will. It's over. And the sooner you accept that, the better off we'll both be," Sandy said firmly.

"I'm not going to let you go, Sandy," Roland said stubbornly. "You may think you can dismiss me that easily, but you're mistaken." He rose. His green eyes had darkened. "I'll be back, again and again, until you'll have no choice but to let me back into your life. I don't have any reason to give up, but every reason to persist. I want you back, Sandy. You're all I think about day and night."

With that, he strode away. Sandy sat shaken, her little speech sticking in her throat.

He hadn't really heard a word she'd said. He was intent on one thing, reclaiming what he thought was rightfully his. And he was obviously determined in his quest.

* * *

Sandy's life became bleak. Old fears and anxieties welled up in her at unexpected moments. Despair and confusion troubled her constantly.

She had dreams from which she awoke bathed in perspiration, her heart pounding wildly. Her work suffered. She could no longer concentrate. She became snappy and short-tempered.

Would she have to live like this forever? she wondered. There was no way she could endure the emotional torment.

She couldn't think rationally where Roland was concerned. In spite of her new insights about him and their marriage, she couldn't shake a feeling of brooding oppression. Roland was too unpredictable, too volatile for her ever to relax. She was slipping into a state of depression.

There was only one thing left to do. She would have to run again. She could sneak out of town. She would do as she had on the trip to New York. She would take only a few pieces of luggage. Roland would think she was off on a buying trip.

She would leave all her furniture behind in her apartment. She would pay her utility bills and her rent for the next month. By the time Roland figured out she wasn't coming back, she'd be halfway across the country, settled in some small town. She would fool him this time. He would look for her in the big city. But she'd be in a small community somewhere, a place where strangers stuck out. If he tracked her down, she'd know it before he found her.

She was going to have to tell her mother the truth. She hated to shatter her mother's feeling of security, but there was no way she could just disappear and not let her mother know where she had gone.

The next morning, Sandy entered Carl Van Helmut's office and handed him a slender white envelope.

"What's this?" he asked, taking it in his hand.

"My resignation," she said stonily.

Chapter Ten

$\mathcal{A}$ chill spread through the room. A suffocating silence overcame Sandy. Weakly she sank into the nearest chair.

Carl Van Helmut looked at the letter in his hand.

"Can't take the heat, huh?" he asked. She didn't like the accusing tone.

She wanted to blurt out the real reason for her departure. She wanted to shout that she could handle her job better than even she had suspected. But the words refused to come.

She shot him a helpless look and said nothing.

"Is it me or the job?" he asked, tossing the envelope on the desk. He stood up, his height dwarfing the desk, and strode around to face her.

"Neither," Sandy said. "I just decided it's time to move on."

"Sandy, that doesn't make any sense," Carl said

bluntly. "You practically begged me for the buyer's job. You've been on one trip. Your merchandise hasn't even begun to arrive yet. I know you better than you think I do. You're the type who doesn't run out in the middle of the second act of the play. You know you want to stick around and see how your selections sell. So why the letter of resignation? What's the real reason?"

There was a note of caring in his voice. Sandy looked up at him. A strange sensation seeped through her. It was as if she were seeing Carl for the first time. His voice rang with genuine concern for her.

How different he was from Roland. Roland thought only about himself, about what he wanted, what he needed. But Carl was obviously interested in her problem, in why she was leaving.

If only she could tear down the protective wall she had built around herself. But she was too frightened. Besides, Carl had never said anything about loving her. Attraction did not equal love.

She stared at him wordlessly.

"Sandy, it's not professional for you to leave like this. If you let what's happened between us force you to resign . . . It was never my intention to lose you as an employee. . . . Sandy, do you realize what you're doing?" His voice had grown soft, compassionate.

"I know what I'm doing," she choked.

"But why? Won't you tell me? Let me help you."

"It's too late for that," she said. "My mind's made up. But I don't want anyone else to know. Let me tell my own department. It's important to me that no one know just yet."

She couldn't take a chance that Roland might

question some of her friends and discover she was quitting.

"All right," Carl said slowly. "If that's the way you want it. At least you've been decent enough to give two weeks' notice. I guess a store can't expect more loyalty than that from its employees." He sounded bitter.

Sandy left Carl's office as fast as she could. Fear and depression threatened to overwhelm her. She didn't want to resign, but she had no choice.

She didn't know where she was going or how she would say goodbye to her mother and Julia. She didn't know anything except that she had to run again, to run as fast and as far as she could before Roland found out her plan.

That Friday, Sandy left her department in a state of dejection. She had worked so hard to make something of herself. And Roland had come along to destroy it all. It wasn't fair!

But all her anger and hostility climaxed when she climbed the back stairs to her apartment and ran face to face into Roland!

She should have known he'd approach her again. But she was hoping to be gone by the time he made another attempt to talk to her.

A feeling of helplessness smothered her. She gathered all her resources to conquer it, and she jutted out her chin defiantly.

"What do you want?" she demanded.

"Just to see you," he said.

He stood in the shadows, his face almost hidden in the darkness.

He reached out toward her.

She moved back.

"I just want to touch you," he pleaded. "Do you

know how long it's been since I've felt a woman's skin? He ran his hand down her arm.

She shuddered, closing her eyes. "I'm busy," she said, opening her eyes and shooting him a belligerent look.

"Sandy, you might as well make up your mind to start seeing me again. I'm not going to leave you alone. My life means nothing without you."

"I don't have time to talk to you now!" Sandy cried, brushing past him. She ran the rest of the way down the hall. She rushed into her apartment and slammed the door behind her, leaning against it and crying.

The silence was broken by a scrape of footsteps outside her door. Sandy caught her breath. Exhaling became impossible. The footsteps plodded back and forth, back and forth.

So this was how he would try to wear down her resistance. He'd drive her so batty with his constant presence that she'd give in just to retain her sanity.

Tears slipped from her eyelids and streamed down her face.

"Dear God, please make him go away!" she whispered.

The footsteps finally ceased. Frantically, Sandy ran to her closet and ripped out her suitcase. Blindly, she flung her clothes into it, not knowing or caring what she was grabbing.

Panic and near hysteria drove her. She would have to leave now, to run as soon as she thought Roland was gone. She had been foolish to think she should give two weeks' notice to the store. What did her integrity matter under the circumstances?

Sandy lost all track of time. She paced the floor, frantic to look in the hallway to see if Roland had actually left, but afraid he might be there waiting for her.

Suddenly, there was a rap on the door. Her heart lurched in her chest.

There was a pause. The knock came again, louder and more insistent.

Sandy stared mutely at the door. She backed away from it, as if doing so would somehow protect her.

"Sandy, are you in there?" came a female voice. "It's me, Julia. I need to talk to you."

A rush of relief flooded over her. A dam somewhere inside her broke, and the tension melted out of her. Along with it came a rush of fresh tears. Sandy hurried to the door and let Julia in.

Julia put her arms around Sandy, hugging her, patting her on the back. "Sandy, what's going on?" she asked, pushing Sandy away from her and giving her a quizzical look. "I heard you were leaving the store. I don't understand."

"You heard . . . what?" Sandy choked. She sat weakly on the couch. Julia took a place beside her.

"It's supposed to be some kind of big secret. Deanna was in Carl's office the other afternoon waiting to talk to him. Apparently, in addition to her other sterling qualities, she's also a snoop. She saw a letter on his desk from you, turning in your resignation. When he came in, she hinted around about it, but he said nothing, so she figured it was top secret. However, that didn't keep her from telling everyone within ten miles. I thought you ought to know. Besides, I have to admit I'm a little hurt you didn't tell me. I thought we were friends."

"Oh, Julia, we are," Sandy said morosely. "I've just been under so much pressure I haven't known what to do. I just wanted to sneak away."

"Why, Sandy? What's the matter?"

"Julia, I need to talk to someone. I'm about to explode keeping this all to myself. I'm not sure it's fair to burden you with my problems, but I know I haven't been fair to you not to confide in you. Either way, I feel so awful."

"Sandy, I've known for a long time something has been troubling you, something more than you've told me. Maybe there's a way I can help if you'll tell me the whole story. Why don't you give it a try?"

"Oh, Julia, you're so kind. I don't deserve a friend like you. There's nothing you can do to help. But I want you to know what's happened so you'll understand why I have to leave, why I've been so nervous and upset lately."

So Sandy spent the evening telling Julia the whole story of her marriage to Roland. She left nothing out. She recalled how Roland had first captured her heart with his flattery, how he had painted her portrait and won over her mother. She told about her early marriage, how happy they'd been, how blind she'd been to subtle signs of Roland's true character.

She described Roland's work and the flashes of genius that eluded him so much of the time.

She also told how the marriage had become troubled, how Roland took out his frustration and sense of inadequacy on her, accusing her of being a poor wife, a stupid hick who understood nothing of art and culture. She told of her growing feeling of despair and helpless uncertainty.

It was difficult to describe Roland's bouts with the bottle. Even harder was the story of how he had beaten Sandy, especially the last time.

"It was over his paintings." She shuddered. "He had got a special commission to produce several works and felt it was the start of an important phase of his career. He roughed me up a little bit and knocked me into one of the canvases. I tried to catch myself, but when I did, I stumbled into two other paintings that were drying. I made a real mess of them. They were scattered all over the room, absolutely ruined. Roland flew into a rage."

The saddest and most wrenching part of the tale was admitting she'd stayed with him too long. Roland's mistreatment caused her to lose her baby.

"I—I was too much of a kid then to really know what to do. I didn't know about things like women's shelters. I was too humiliated and ashamed to tell my mother about my marriage problems, and then it was too late. . . ."

When she finished, she felt drained. A great sadness settled on her, and she sat back against the couch and closed her eyes, grateful for the sense of release.

"I understand so many things about you now that had been a mystery to me," Julia said softly. "In your place, I would have felt the same way."

Sandy smiled weakly. "I knew if anyone would understand, you would."

"And what about Carl?" Julia asked. "I know it wouldn't be easy for you to learn to love and trust again, Sandy, but Carl is such a different person from Roland. I know the family. They're a little stern, but underneath they're kind, compassionate and caring. It would be a shame to let what happened with Roland destroy your chances for happiness with Carl. You can pick up the pieces and go on,

Sandy. The right man can do wonders to help you. Carl might just be that man, if you'd give him a chance."

"I can't, Julia," Sandy said in a monotone. "I just want to get away from here, to start my life over again. And now I'm so very tired. Will you stay for a while? I don't want to be alone right now."

"Sure," Julia said warmly. "I'll stay."

"Thanks," Sandy said. Wearily she pulled herself up from the couch and headed for the bedroom. "I'm going to rest for a while. Then we'll have something to eat, OK?"

"Fine," Julia said. "I'll just read a book or a magazine or something. You go ahead."

Sandy went into the bedroom and stretched herself out across the bed. A little nap would do wonders for her, she thought groggily. She was so tired. . . .

She didn't know what time it was when she awoke. She felt disoriented. Perplexed, she looked around the room. It was dark and she was fully clothed. Where was she? What had happened?

Then her memory returned to her. She had fallen into an exhausted sleep. She had been emotionally drained from her long conversation with Julia. She had taken a nap, but how long had she slept?

Sandy shook her head to clear it. Then she glanced at her watch. It was ten o'clock! Too late to skip town tonight, she thought dismally. She'd have to wait until morning.

She sat up, stuck her tongue out from the bad taste in her mouth and decided the first order of business was to get herself together. She went into the bathroom, brushed her teeth, pulled a brush through her long blond hair and straightened her clothes.

Julia must be famished, she thought to herself.

Sandy walked to the living room. "Are you ready to eat a late supper?" she said. But instead of finding Julia sitting on the couch, she found Carl Van Helmut!

"W-what are you doing here?" Sandy gasped.

"Julia called me," he said, standing. His expression was soft, concerned. His voice was compassionate. His blue eyes found hers and said he knew.

Anger and humiliation overcame her. "She had no right!"

"She knew she was taking a chance with your friendship, but she said it was better to lose you as a friend than to have you take off again and never see you. She did what she thought was best for you, Sandy."

"How can telling you help me?" Sandy demanded. "How much did she tell you?"

"The whole story, Sandy."

She sighed. "So you know all the lovely little details of my past. They have a name for unfortunate women like me—I was a battered wife," she whispered bitterly.

He took her hand in his. She flinched. He pulled her down onto the couch beside him.

"Now I understand so many things about you," Carl went on. "You're really something. You persevered in spite of tremendous odds against you. You've made something of yourself, Sandy. You didn't go off whimpering in a corner and lick your wounds and wait for somebody to put you back together. There are many people in this world who are losers because they think life dealt them a rotten hand. All they can do is complain and pout and expect life to make it up to them. They never try to fight back. It's a hard world out there, and the winners are those people who kick life in the rear end and refuse to go down without a fight.

"Sure, we all bear some scars from life's blows, but nobody gets through this existence unscathed. It happens to everybody eventually in one form or another. And I admire you, Sandy, because you had the guts to fight back."

She forced herself to look at him. His blue eyes were glittering. Surprised, she saw admiration in his eyes.

Carl Van Helmut was a winner. He had licked life's obstacles. And he admired another person who had done the same. But admiration and love were not the same thing.

"Yeah, I fought back," she said. She felt weary again. "But what good did it do me? My ex-husband is back in my life again, and it's a replay of the same problem. Only this time I know what to expect from him. And the only solution is to go somewhere so he can't find me."

"You could run." Carl nodded slowly. He was thoughtful for a moment, then quietly dropped a bombshell. "Or . . . you could get married."

She stared at him, bewildered, not sure she heard right.

"What are you talking about?"

"From what Julia told me, your ex-husband apparently thinks he has a chance to make you come back to him because you're still single. If he's the type I suspect he is, he'll keep hounding you. But a manly confrontation would change his mind. If you married, he'd have to realize it was over between you two, that he's out of your life for good. He wouldn't dare bother you if you had a husband to protect you. His type is basically a coward; that's why he takes his anger and frustration out on somebody weaker than himself."

"That may all be true, but it would be a little hard for me to drum up a husband on the spur of the moment," Sandy said wryly.

"Maybe not," Carl said. "I'll marry you."

She stared at him speechlessly, then choked, "W-what?"

"I said I'll marry you."

"You have to be kidding!"

"No. I'm serious, Sandy."

She was dumbfounded.

"But—but why?" she stammered. Then a glimmer of hope twinkled in her. Was he using this devious method to tell her he loved her?

She examined her feelings for him. If he declared his love for her, how would she respond? She felt toward Carl as she had never felt toward any man in her life. It was love, she was sure of it, but it was so buried under her fear of men that she had never been able to confront it. She wanted to hold the feeling in her heart, to savor it, to wrap herself in the blanket of its warmth. But always there was a wall of fear preventing her from admitting to herself her deepest longings.

If Carl said the words she yearned, yet feared, to hear, would that icy wall crumble at last?

"Why?" Carl repeated slowly. "I'm not sure, Sandy. Do I love you? I've asked myself that question. I'm attracted to you, but I don't know yet how deep my feelings for you really go, or how deep they can go."

He hesitated, then said, "Sandy, it may look to you as if I was born with a silver spoon in my mouth, but you don't know the real struggle I had. As a result, I've become rather hardened. But I feel a softness toward you, Sandy. I've never felt this way toward another woman.

"I can't define it as love. I don't know where it will lead. I don't even know if I'm capable of love."

He leaned forward, resting his elbows on his legs. He rubbed his hands together.

Sandy gazed at him steadily. He blinked several times as if gathering his scattered thoughts.

Then he continued, "But I do care for you. I desire you. At the same time, I want to take care of you. I don't know if I'm making a whole lot of sense to you . . . or to myself!" He made a gesture that indicated his frustration at putting his complex emotions into words.

Giving up any further attempt to analyze his motives, he said bluntly, "Look, Sandy, if you'll marry me, I'll treat you decently. You won't have to worry about Roland hounding you anymore. And if the marriage just doesn't work out . . . if we give it a try and you decide you're unhappy with me, I won't create any problems about granting you a divorce any time you wish."

Carl's words had left her bewildered and shaken. She had not in her wildest dreams anticipated this development. There was such a sense of unreality about the turn of events that she felt dazed, unable to formulate any clear thoughts. She felt desperately weary. She was so tired of living in a state of uncertainty and fear! The offer of strong arms to shield her was overwhelmingly tempting.

Carl's concern for her seemed real. But could she

be sure; could she trust him? She knew some things about him and yet there was much she didn't know. Carl did have a hard, ruthless side to his nature, perhaps a result of the struggles he'd had in his own lifetime. In some ways he had remained very much a stranger to her.

Yes, she would be taking a chance with Carl. But not as great a chance as she would with Roland persistently intruding on her life. Her emotions couldn't take any more of that!

She drew a deep breath. Her eyes met Carl's. Slowly, she nodded.

She felt Carl's strong hand grip hers.

Chapter Eleven

A big, formal wedding?" Sandy stared at Carl aghast. "Surely you're not serious!"

Carl smiled tolerantly. "But why not, Sandy?"

"Lots of reasons," Sandy gasped.

It was the next morning in Carl's office. They had not discussed the wedding plans the night before. Sandy had been too stunned by Carl's startling and unorthodox proposal to make any rational plans. Carl had been considerate enough to let her have a night's sleep so she could adjust to the situation. But he had sent word when she arrived for work that he wanted to see her in his office. And he had proceeded to drop this new bombshell.

"Yes, there are plenty of good reasons I don't want a big, elaborate wedding," Sandy exclaimed, rising from her chair and pacing about the office nervously. "Carl, I'm surprised you'd even suggest it under the circumstances."

"I don't know why you find it so startling," Carl said with infuriating calmness. "It seems perfectly logical to me."

"Logical?"

"Certainly. I don't mean to put on airs or sound like a social snob, but let's face facts. In this city, when a Van Helmut gets married, it's bound to cause quite a stir in social circles. It really wouldn't be fair to my family and all their friends for us not to include them all."

"But," Sandy spluttered, "I'd feel like a terrible hypocrite!"

Carl raised an eyebrow questioningly.

"All right, as you said, let's face facts. This isn't exactly a match made in heaven. You told me quite frankly that you're not sure if you love me or would ever be in love with me. You've desired me for some time, and you've seized on this opportunity to get me to marry you, only because you've decided it's the only way you can get me to go to bed with you."

Carl flushed. His eyes flashed angrily.

But before he could speak, she hurriedly added, "Carl, I know you're also doing this out of a sincere desire to protect me from this ugly situation with my ex-husband, and I want you to know I appreciate that from the very bottom of my heart. But all that doesn't add up to the reason people usually get married."

"Which is?"

"Because they love one another, of course. Because they want to establish a home and perhaps raise a family. Because they want to be together . . . to grow old together—" Her voice broke. She was dangerously close to tears.

Carl shrugged. There was an air of detachment

about him. "I suppose I'm not a very sentimental person. It appears to me, looking at the divorce rate, that all those lofty and mushy notions about romantic intoxication aren't much of a guarantee the thing will work out."

Sandy flashed him an angry look. "Well, I'm sorry," she said coldly. "I happen to have the old-fashioned notion that love is very important. And that's why I feel that it would almost be a sacrilege to have a big, elaborate church wedding in our circumstances."

Then she added, "But all right, putting sentiment and ideals aside, there's the very practical reason that I couldn't begin to afford such a wedding. The cost of a wedding is borne by the bride's family, as you know. My mother doesn't have that kind of money, even with all the financial help I'd be able to give her—"

"Well, of course I understand that," Carl said, "and I would certainly take care of all expenses. I naturally wouldn't expect you to pay for this kind of wedding. As a matter of fact, my parents want to pick up the tab. They want it to be part of their wedding present to us."

For a moment, Sandy was unable to speak. "That's—that's very sweet of them," she stammered. "I'm touched. But I really don't want to go through the ordeal of such a fancy wedding, Carl. . . ."

He chewed his lip thoughtfully. "Sandy, try looking at it this way. You're very loyal to the business. I know the store is as important to you as it is to me. Think of the valuable publicity Van Helmut's could gain from this kind of wedding. 'Heir to Van Helmut

Fortune Marries Store Employee.' A natural news story. We could play up the event in our ads."

She stared at him, her emotions churning. If she needed any further proof of Carl's detached attitude toward their union, this was certainly it. As far as he was concerned, it was entirely a matter of practical arrangement, a kind of business deal that would benefit both of them. She would be forever rid of Roland's dark shadow over her life. As for Carl, he'd get what he'd desired for some time: her body. And while he was about it, why not a little extra profit for the store!

But nowhere in his argument had he said anything about love. Perhaps it would not hurt so much if she could be as detached about him as he apparently was about her. But though she fought against admitting it to herself even now, she realized that Carl Van Helmut was a dangerous threat to the wall she had maintained so long around her heart.

She tried a final, and what she thought would be a convincing, argument. "It would be in poor taste for me to walk down the aisle at a big, formal wedding in a white gown. Remember, I've been married before."

But Carl dismissed that argument with a wave of his hand. "In today's society, with so many divorced people remarrying, that old rule is often set aside. Anyway, I doubt if anyone except Julia and I know about your former marriage. If other people do find out and raise a few eyebrows, so what?" He shrugged. "It means nothing to me."

She gazed at him, at his carelessly combed shock of blond hair, his blue eyes that could search her inner being with devastating force, his lean, athletic body and broad shoulders, and she felt something become weak and trembling inside her. She flushed and looked away. Then she sighed and bowed her head in submission. "All right, Carl. If it means that much to you . . ."

The weeks that followed plunged Sandy into hectic preparations for the elaborate wedding that seemed so important to the Van Helmut family. She was feted with bridal showers. Wherever she went in the store, she drew intense and envious stares, much to her discomfort. She read her name in the social columns of the newspaper and wondered, with a sense of unreality, if it were all some kind of dream from which she would awaken at any moment.

But the dream did not end. And soon the big day came when she stood at the back of the church and the great organ began the wedding march, signaling the beginning of a whole new life for her.

She glanced down for a final, nervous inspection of her gown, the most exquisitely designed and the most costly that the Van Helmut store could provide. When she moved, there was a soft, luxurious rustle of the finest combination of Chantilly laces. The V-neck was encrusted with tiny seed pearls in a scroll figuration. The lace sleeves were Bishop in design while the yoke was sheer, and the bodice had been created with a wide V-shaped trim of reembroidered Chantilly lace. A narrow satin ribbon trimmed with Venice lace motifs defined the empire waistline. The skirt, all lace and three-tiered, was fashioned with a ruffled hemline. And there was a formal chapel train. The final touch was a Camelot headpiece that held a lace-trimmed illusion that fell in a gentle mist to her fingertips.

Her self-conscious attention moved from her elegant gown to the sea of humanity that filled the great church. It appeared that the Van Helmuts knew, and had invited, everyone of importance in the Southwest. Carl had mentioned that an ex-governor, several congressmen, a Washington columnist and numerous other VIPs would attend the wedding and reception along with a multitude of the Van Helmuts' friends and relatives.

Sandy experienced a suffocating wave of stage fright. She clutched the strong arm of Otto Van Helmut for support as her legs trembled. The old man patted her hand reassuringly.

Not having a father or another male relative to give her away, she had asked Carl's father to do the honors. He had accepted with pride and delight.

Today his ruddy face beamed and his blue eyes glittered behind gold-rimmed spectacles. Except for a slight limp, his health problems appeared to be much improved. Getting both his sons married had acted like a tonic for his emotions.

Just before the wedding march began, Otto had murmured to Sandy, "You and I had our differences when I was running the store, Sandy. I thought you were a little too hard, too aggressive. But that's just the kind of woman for my son, Carl . . . one with some spunk and backbone, one who'll stand up to him." The old man grinned. "Both my sons have made me happy. They've picked good women for themselves. You're going to make a fine daughter-in-law, Sandy. You'll fit right into the family with your background in the business. You and Carl will take up where I left off. The business will grow in your hands. Yes, both boys have done me proud."

Sandy was deeply moved at the warm welcome

into the Van Helmut family that she had been given by both Carl's father and mother. Their sincerity had increased her qualms and uncertainty at the step she was taking. What if the members of this fine old family knew the real reasons she and Carl were getting married? Her cheeks flushed with humiliation. She made a silent vow that she would try with all her heart to become a good wife for Carl, though she knew she was facing a bitter struggle. She was marrying an aloof and enigmatic man who had made it quite clear that he was not marrying her because he loved her. No matter how she felt about him, could she really live with a man under those circumstances?

Otto squeezed her hand again and nodded, indicating it was time for the wedding procession to start down the aisle.

Sandy made a frantic effort to gain control of her thoughts, which were scattering in all directions. She forced herself to picture every detail of the rehearsal.

First they had decided on the best tempo at which to have the wedding march played. The ushers had stepped off down the aisle while Sandy, her mother and the Van Helmuts had judged the effect. Too slow would make it look like a funeral, while too fast would be ridiculous.

Then the entire procession had practiced their entrance and march down the aisle. It was arranged by height: First came the two shorter ushers followed by the junior bridesmaids; then the bridesmaids; the maid of honor—who was Sandy's best friend, Julia—walking alone; then the children, all great-nieces and great-nephews of the senior Van

Helmuts; the flower girls, and the ring bearer. Then Otto Van Helmut had come with a cousin of Carl's who was the bride's stand-in, and finally two chubby, giggling four-year-old boys who would be the pages holding the bride's train.

The rehearsal had gone smoothly. But this was the real thing. There was no stand-in for the bride, no make-believe. This was she, Sandy Carver, playing the real-life part, going to meet the man who in a few minutes would be her husband.

She glanced at the feet of those preceding her, remembering to get in step with them, mentally saying to herself, "Left, left . . ."

The flower girls, sprinkling rose petals in her path, and the ring bearer, a darling three-year-old girl proudly carrying the ring on a pink satin cushion, had started down the aisle. Sandy counted eight beats, then she and Otto Van Helmut started together, each on his or her left foot. She mentally repeated the instructions of the bridal consultant. "Try to walk as naturally as possible, but keep in step with the music and keep the same distance from those in front of you. Most brides are so nervous it takes a considerable amount of self-control not to rush things."

Sandy felt as if she were seeing the procession through a mist. The gowns of the bridesmaids were a sea of blue, but in graduated hues. The first two were a deep, aquamarine blue. The next two wore gowns of a more delicate, sky-blue tint, and the two that followed wore a shade lighter still. Finally, Julia's gown was a fragile shade of robin's-egg blue.

The bridesmaids carried bouquets of roses.

Then Sandy caught sight of Carl for the first time

that day. He, with his best man and ushers, was waiting at the altar. She felt the impact of his intense gaze across the distance. It took her breath away.

Since it was a daytime wedding, the men were dressed in gray-striped trousers, cutaway coats and single-breasted black waistcoats. Carl looked dashing and handsome in the formal attire. He appeared quite at ease, accustomed to such protocol, while Sandy felt painfully self-conscious and uncertain.

Then she was at his side. She heard the solemn words of the marriage ceremony. In a daze, she felt the cold band of the wedding ring encircle her finger. The minister spoke the final words of the ceremony: "I now pronounce you man and wife." Carl's strong arms swept her close to him. His gaze searched her eyes with a look of proud possession. Then his kiss burned her lips.

She was vaguely aware of the flash of the photographer's camera. The triumphant sounds of the recessional pealed through the sanctuary. Carl took her arm and they led the wedding party back down the aisle. Rows of smiling faces greeted her. For the first time she saw her mother, bleary-eyed but smiling. She felt a stab of remorse for the worry and pain her first marriage had caused her mother. Would it be any different this time? Already doubts and uncertainties were assailing her.

She recalled the night she had broken the news of her engagement to her mother. She had invited Carl, Julia and Brut to her apartment for supper and had included her mother. It was the first time her mother was introduced to Carl.

He had been gracious to her, but the evening had been strained. Sandy's mother had been shy and ill at ease.

Later she told Sandy, "I'm sure he's a very fine man, but I don't know how to act around people like the Van Helmuts. I'm just a simple woman from a small town, Sandy. You've moved up in the world, I guess. . . ."

Her mother had looked at her with a mingling of pride and regret, as if suddenly aware that they were no longer as close as they once had been. Sandy tried to reassure her mother by hugging her and telling her that nothing would ever change her love for her. But at the same time she realized that it was true; she had come a long way from her small-town background, into the fast-paced, competitive world of garment merchandising. Her ambitious drive had been a defense, a kind of escape and compensation for the tragedy of her first marriage. Somewhere along the way she had changed. She was no longer the same trusting, innocent young girl who had taken her marriage vows that first time; Roland had seen to that. Right now she wasn't quite sure who she was. The air of confidence she portrayed at her job only disguised her deep uncertainty . . . an uncertainty that now included her relationship with Carl Van Helmut.

Her mother had squeezed her hand that night. "Don't let what I say upset you, Sandy. I just want you to be happy."

"Thank you, Mother. I am happy. . . ."

She hoped her voice sounded more confident than she felt. Now she was no longer Sandy Carver. She was Mrs. Carl Van Helmut. She repeated the name in her mind, trying to grasp the reality of it.

The wedding party remained at the church for more photographs, then they went on to the reception, which was being catered at one of Houston's posh country clubs.

True to the style of the Van Helmuts, the reception had been planned with a flair of extravagance. At one end of the spacious ballroom, a series of tables were bedecked with gleaming white linen cloths. On one of the tables was a gigantic wedding cake with five tiers. Draped gracefully around the cake and trailing down the table were garlands of pale-lavender orchids.

The buffet table offered a lavish choice of shrimp, *escargots,* caviar, stuffed mushrooms, *seviche,* quiche, French pastries and fresh fruits, all on silver platters nestled on beds of green ferns and white orchids. On another table, at the other end of the room, was the groom's cake, silver coffee urns and stacks of small white boxes, each filled with a slice of cake as a wedding favor. There was a legend that if a guest placed the box of cake under her pillow that night, she would dream of her loved one.

A large, nationally known society orchestra filled the room with smooth melodies.

Sandy stood in the reception line, conscious of Carl's broad shoulders beside her, as a stream of guests filed by offering good wishes and congratulations.

Julia hugged Sandy. "Life is full of surprises." She grinned. "I sure didn't dream you'd beat me down the aisle!"

Brut squeezed her hand, then kissed her. "Welcome to the family, sister-in-law! If you have any trouble keeping big brother in line, let me know and I'll straighten him out."

When the guests had been welcomed, Sandy danced with Carl, signaling the start of the reception festivities. The wedding cake was cut. There was a constant flashing of the photographer's equipment.

At one time during the flurry of activities, Sandy found herself in a quiet corner with Carl's mother. "You look remarkably poised and calm, Sandy," Mrs. Van Helmut observed.

"I do?" Sandy said with surprise.

There was a regal air about the older woman. Her dark-blond hair with its clearly defined widow's peak was styled in a large bun on the back of her head. Her eyes were soft brown, her mouth generous, but Sandy sensed the Van Helmut strength in her character.

"Yes," Mrs. Van Helmut continued, "I would say you have the determination to see yourself through difficult situations. That's an admirable quality. I'm sure a big wedding like this has been a strain."

"Yes, it has," Sandy agreed, wondering if Carl's mother knew how she was teetering on the ragged edge of a nervous collapse. Then she admitted frankly, "You could just be seeing a front I'm putting on."

"Well, if that's true, you're doing an excellent job of covering up. Anyone who saw you would think you were quite at ease and enjoying yourself."

Sandy was aware of the older woman's penetrating scrutiny, and she quickly looked away, wondering with a feeling of consternation if Mrs. Van Helmut suspected the real strain she was under—the peculiar reasons for this marriage. Would she be as friendly if she knew?

Sandy had the sudden thought that her marriage to Carl Van Helmut had the elements of old-world arranged unions where couples married for practical considerations rather than for love.

Her mother-in-law spoke again, interrupting her thoughts. "I think you and Carl will get along fine, my dear. You seem to be cut from the same cloth. My older son has a bit of steel in his makeup, probably from the struggles he had with health problems when he was growing up. I sense that same element in you. I'm not prying into your private life when I say this, Sandy, but my guess is that you've had your own mountains to climb, and it's toughened your moral fiber. I do hope your feelings for Carl are sincere. I know how you've worked your way up through the ranks at the store. I truly hope you're marrying my son because you love him."

Sandy was surprised and disconcerted. The older woman's keen insight was dangerously close to the truth. But then she changed the subject abruptly. Her expression changed, becoming light and animated. "I see your husband is coming to claim another dance with his bride." She squeezed Sandy's hand. "Good luck, my dear. . . ."

Her parting words were soft, almost inaudible. Rather than reassuring her, they added to Sandy's feeling of uncertainty about the future. Was there an element of doubt in the wish . . . a half-spoken prayer to allay her own misgivings?

The reception continued in a smooth fashion. Sandy threw her bouquet to the women, her garter to the men, all in prescribed ritual and protocol. She and Carl departed in a shower of rose petals that had been substituted for the traditional rice. A limousine whisked them to the airport. Sandy had changed into her travel garment, a suit in a toast hue, its simple lines expressing good taste and style. The jacket was cropped, with a button front and contoured bottom. It had front and back princess seaming and padded shoulders. The simplicity of the skirt was fashionably distracted by a clever front-pleating detail. When Sandy had given her appearance a final, full-length mirror check, she realized how much she had learned about style and fashion since she'd traded her small-town background for a career in the merchandising of women's garments.

Carl had told her they were flying to New York for their honeymoon. They would combine business with pleasure, he had explained. While in New York they could visit some specialty showrooms in search of some unique items for their Christmas catalogue. Every year Van Helmut's offered several extravagantly expensive gifts that only the superrich could afford. It was a clever publicity stunt that never failed to get the store some news coverage.

Sandy felt oddly self-conscious and shy with Carl when they were on the plane together. She was acutely aware of the wedding ring. It felt like a hot band around her finger, constantly calling attention to its unfamiliar presence. In contrast to Carl's apparent relaxed, conversational mood, Sandy was withdrawn and ill at ease, her thoughts scattered, her emotions in disarray.

She was shocked when a limousine took them from the airport to the hotel and she found herself in front of the same door she had occupied on her previous buying trip.

"This couldn't be a coincidence," she said, her cheeks flaming.

Carl chuckled. "No."

She shot him a dangerous look, but held her tongue until the bellhop had left the room. When they were alone, she demanded, "Did you do this to embarrass me?"

He raised an eyebrow. "Why would I do that?"

"I have no idea, unless you have a streak of cruelty in you!"

"I still don't understand," he said, looking perplexed.

"You know good and well what happened in this room. How I almost . . . how we—" Her voice spluttered into humiliated silence.

His mocking grin infuriated her even more. "How we came very close to making love?" He asked, gently drawing her into his arms. "How excited and passionate you became?" His voice grew husky. She felt his lips against her hair, then the warmth of his breath against her cheek and neck as his lips trailed downward and he continued to murmur softly, "How we lay on the bed in each other's arms, and how much you wanted me to make love to you. . . ."

Her thoughts were becoming disarrayed again. She felt some of the resistance melting from her body, the stiffness giving away to trembling. She was furious with herself for having no more self-control. "You—you just caught me in a weak moment," she choked. "I do not just go to bed with a man like that. . . ."

"So I found out," he murmured wryly. "But now we are man and wife."

His lips moved closer, touching the flesh of her throat, moving to the hollow of her bosom.

"Carl," she whispered thickly. "No . . . I—I don't think I can. . . ."

"You don't?" he teased. "Then why do I feel your heart beating so hard?"

"Out of fear!"

He gazed deeply into her eyes with a searching,

questioning gaze. Softly he asked, "Fear of what? Fear of your own passion? I know you want me, Sandy . . . as much as I want you, otherwise I would not have married you."

She tried to escape his penetrating gaze. Again she felt warmth rush to her cheeks. "Physical desire has nothing to do with love," she said weakly.

He smiled. "It's a good beginning. And why do I have the feeling that it's not at all one-sided!"

"That sounds like male conceit!"

He simply brushed that protestation aside by scooping her up in his arms and carrying her to the bed. There he slipped the jacket of her suit from her shoulders. She was finding it difficult to breath, a difficulty that increased as he tenderly opened the front of her blouse. The pupils of his eyes expanded as he drank in the delicate secrets of her breasts that were barely hidden by a wispy lace bra. She felt the blood coursing through her arteries in heated surges. Conflict raged in her. The inhibitions that had kept her normal passions locked away for so many years were crumbling. It was both a thrilling and a frightening sensation.

Carl shrugged out of his jacket in a single, fluid movement and tossed it over a chair. But before he could go any further, there was a discreet tap at the door. Sandy came to a sitting position, automatically smoothing her hair and quickly closing her blouse, not sure if she felt relief or disappointment.

With a muttered exclamation, Carl opened the door. It was the bellboy, who wheeled in a bottle of champagne in a silver bucket of ice covered by a white cloth. With a flourish, he turned over two fragile goblets on the silver tray and set them beside the bucket. Carl tipped him generously. He smiled his thanks, shot Sandy a glance that sent a flush of self-conscious warmth racing through her body, then left, closing the door softly behind him.

Carl wrapped the napkin around the chilled bottle and skillfully worked the cork loose with his thumb. The loud *pop* caused Sandy to start. He filled the crystal goblets with the bubbling liquid and handed one to Sandy. She sipped the effervescent wine, coughed and blinked.

"Tickle your nose?"

She nodded. She sat on the edge of the bed, slowly sipping the expensive, imported champagne, aware of its alchemy working to relax her walls of restraint.

Still in an expansive mood, Carl had two glasses of champagne, but when he offered to refill Sandy's glass, she shook her head. Carl smiled teasingly, "Champagne is the drink of lovers. Sure you won't have another?"

She flushed and looked away, wondering if he could sense the fluttering in her stomach.

The bed sagged under the weight of Carl's masculine physique as he sat beside her, leaning against the pillows. His hand brushed her hip as he settled beside her. She drew in her breath sharply.

He entwined the fingers of both hands, clasping them behind his head. She felt his steady gaze on her, but she refused to look at him. They were silent for a long moment. The tension in the air became brittle. Sandy felt compelled to break the uncomfortable silence, but her mind went blank when she tried to think of something to say. Her gaze darted around the room, searching for something on which to focus and came to rest on her own thigh, which was dangerously near Carl's leg. She felt a warmth through her dress where their limbs almost touched, as if she could feel the animal heat radiating from his sinews. Her heart thudded heavily.

Sandy waited for him to speak, but instead of saying anything, he gently picked up her left hand and began tracing a random pattern on its back. A tingling sensation ran up her arm. Gradually, he increased the distance his fingers traveled until soon he was lightly tickling the tender underside of her forearm.

The soothing caress relaxed her and her strained posture gave way to a more comfortable position.

"Feel good?" Carl murmured, his low voice as soothing as the hypnotic caress of his fingers.

Sandy nodded with her eyes closed. "Ummm," she replied.

For long moments Carl continued stroking her arm, then he stopped.

Drowsily she opened her eyes. She was disturbingly aware of how masculine Carl was. His thick blond hair was a bit mussed. There was a rugged balance between his strong jaw and straight nose. In the shadowy light from a table lamp, his cheeks had the glint of bronze.

He removed his tie and tossed it over the chair that held his coat. "Would you like to get more comfortable?" he suggested.

"I—I don't have a tie," she said, attempting a feeble joke.

"No, but you're wearing shoes. Here, allow me."

He caught a finger in the strap of her high-heeled sandal, slipped it off her foot and did the same with the other. A strange shiver ran through her.

His masculine smells filtered through her senses, the mixture of shaving lotion, leather, tobacco and wool.

He reached toward her, touched her hair. Then his touch trailed down to her face, traced the outline of her lips, her jaw, touched the hollow of her throat, then roamed over the buttons of her blouse. Sandy swallowed hard, gazing at him with the expression of a trapped doe.

He smiled reassuringly. "Since your shoes are off, perhaps you'd like a foot rub?"

"A—a foot rub?"

"Sure. Don't tell me you've never had a real, honest to goodness foot rub by an expert."

"Well . . . I—I don't know. I guess not. . . ."

"Then you don't know what you've missed all your life." He chuckled. "I can promise the best foot rub in town. I learned how from my mother, who learned the method from an aunt in the old country. There's a whole method of treating ills by massaging and pressing certain areas of the foot. It's called reflexology. Ever hear of it?"

"No."

"I think the Chinese invented it. Maybe not . . . but they're given credit for so many things. I can remember way back when I was a little kid, when I came home crying from getting a bad grade at school or coming down with some childhood ailment, the way my mother could make me feel better all over with a loving foot rub."

"Perhaps" Sandy said, with a slight catch in her voice, "it was more the love than the rub."

If Carl was aware of the twinge of bitterness in what she said, he did not show it. He merely shrugged, "Perhaps. I'm sure there was as much psychology involved as anything, but there certainly are a lot of nerve endings in one's feet, and the right kind of massage seems to have therapeutic value."

He gently pushed Sandy into a reclining position and placed her feet on his lap. Strong hands went to work. Firm fingers pressed and rubbed.

"There are all sorts of nerves that travel throughout the body, and they all end here." Carl talked in low, soothing tones as he rubbed. "Right here in the feet. Massage the appropriate nerve and distant areas of the body both relax and receive beneficial stimulation."

She couldn't be sure if Carl had learned all this from family folklore or if he were simply making the whole thing up. But she couldn't deny the warm sensations radiating up from her feet throughout her body.

Sandy closed her eyes and surrendered to the delicious feelings that washed over her. Carl certainly seemed to know what he was doing. Anxieties floated away. A calm relaxation blanketed her. For the first time, the misgivings and doubts became suffused and muffled.

Carl worked on her feet and calves for a long time, just how long she neither knew or cared.

After a while, in her dreamy state, she heard him murmur, "I'm pretty good at backs, too. Care to give it a try?"

She no longer had the desire to open her eyes. She simply sighed.

Strong hands gently rolled her over. For a while his fingers moved up and down her spine, touching her through the fabric of her blouse. Then he said softly, "I could do a better job without this in the way."

Before she was fully aware of what was happening, he had reached under her and had unbuttoned her blouse. She seemed incapable of resistance, as if her muscles had turned to butter as he removed her blouse. She felt small and cared for, like a child being put to bed.

But the sensations that tingled through her body as his hands came in contact with the bare flesh of her back were not those of a child. Only a woman whose normal desires had been so long bottled up could experience the flames that began licking through her body.

Vaguely, she was aware of Carl's quickened breath. Skillfully, his caresses moved from her back to her sides and slipped under her bosom, cupping the fullness of her throbbing breasts.

A mounting storm of emotion wiped thought processes from her mind. Gone for the moment were her concerns and reservations about the marriage. In the consuming heat of passion, she was able to forget the pain of loving a man who did not love her in return.

Yes, she was in love with him!

Recklessly, wildly, she admitted it to herself. For how long she didn't know. Perhaps she had fallen in love with him on the previous trip to New York, the buying trip that had placed her in this very bed with him. Or, more likely, it had started before that. When? During their first confrontation in his office? The first time she had seen him?

She didn't know . . . perhaps would never know. All that mattered now was that she cared so much for him that inhibitions and fears were swept away. She could only fill her mind with him, with his strong arms, his broad shoulders, his face. She had memorized every line of his face, the strong, stubborn chin, the mouth that could be both stern and tender, the eyes with their penetrating gaze that could search hers so ruthlessly.

She was too confused to understand why she had fallen in love with Carl. Love for a man had been such an alien experience for her for so many years that she could neither fully comprehend nor trust the emotion. It was simply a fact she could not deny. In a saner moment, she probably could not admit it to herself. But in this moment of passion, sanity was not a factor. She could only cling to this strong, masculine man who was making love to her with such abandon, and in the wildness of the moment could only think to herself, I love you! I love you!

His kisses tasted her lips, demanded that they part so his tongue could find hers. His caresses were everywhere, lighting flash fires where they touched her bare flesh. His lips moved to her throat, down her body to her breasts. Her fingers clutched his hair. She gasped.

The room became silent except for their breathing and gasped exclamations and the rustle of the bed. She gloried in the sensations that swept through her, wave after wave. The universe became centered in a momentous, exploding crescendo of fulfillment. Her body moved feverishly and trembled against him in a spasm of delight.

Then the storm subsided. The waves calmed. Rational thought returned and with it came creeping the same old dark questions. The man beside her became a stranger again. A pleasant, attractive stranger, but a stranger nonetheless.

Carl was relaxed beside her, propped against the pillows, sipping another glass of champagne. He looked flushed and content. But what was he thinking? What was he really like inside? Obviously he hadn't been disappointed with their wedding night. But would he grow tired of the chase now that he'd conquered his prey? She wasn't deluding herself. He had married her to get her in bed with him. Well, he'd done that.

In spite of herself, she felt her old distrust and fear of men seeping into her consciousness like cold, slimy tendrils slithering from some dark cellar of her mind. Almost instinctively, she moved a few inches away from Carl. She looked at him warily, wishing she could penetrate the outer surface of the man, to know his true being. But then she thought it might be better to leave him a stranger. She might not like what she discovered if she swept aside his reserve.

Carl was talking in a pleasant, conversational voice about business, his plans for the store, the things he hoped to accomplish while they were in New York. It was as if they weren't lying here naked, as if they hadn't made love at all. It was just as well, Sandy thought, drawing the sheet up to cover herself. She felt on much safer ground, talking about the business. It would have made her painfully uncomfortable for the conversation to become too personal at this point.

Their week in New York was pleasant enough. Their days were divided between making business calls and sightseeing. They visited museums, took in a Broadway play, ate foreign dishes in out-of-the way restaurants, strolled through Rockefeller Plaza and watched the ice skaters. And at night they made love.

Carl was an enjoyable companion. But he made

no effort to lower the barriers of his reserve. Except when they were in bed, he was like a polite stranger.

They talked very little on the flight back to Houston. Carl was busy with a briefcase of business papers. Sandy leafed through fashion magazines, but she was scarcely aware of what she was reading. Her thoughts were occupied with her uncertain future.

Back in Houston, Sandy moved into Carl's large home. But it was a bittersweet experience. Finally, she was to be mistress of a beautiful home, to have household help, to be recognized as the wife of a respectable man. It was all any woman could ask for, except that her husband didn't love her.

They were good in bed together, but she knew there should be more to a marriage than the bedroom. She knew there should be mutual love binding husband and wife in a lifelong commitment to each other. Sandy could hardly contain her tears as she looked around her plush surroundings. Waves of remorse washed over her. A deep longing filled an aching pit in her stomach.

However, she reminded herself that she had no right to expect anything more than she had. She had agreed to marry Carl knowing he didn't love her. She had sought refuge from Roland in Carl's marriage proposal. For whatever reason, she was using Carl. She realized he was using her, too, but just why, she didn't know.

There was one difference, though. She loved Carl. What had begun as a convenient way out of a complicated situation had turned into a more tangled web than she had ever dreamed she could weave.

How had she gotten herself into this dilemma?

Her mind ran back through the events of the past few days: the wedding, the trip to New York . . . When had she actually fallen in love with Carl? How had it happened? Had she loved him in the deepest recesses of her heart even before the marriage ceremony? Was that why she had agreed to marry him?

Or had it taken place on their honeymoon? After their lovemaking in New York, she had lain in Carl's arms for a time, peaceful and content. But when the glow wore off, she realized what she had done. She had given herself to a man she couldn't understand and really didn't know, a man who at times seemed stern and arrogant.

Carl had been tender and considerate in bed. But still he had made no mention of love. And why should he? He'd made it clear when he proposed that he didn't love her.

Sandy had been so careful for years to preserve the steel barrier that shielded her from entanglements with men. Somehow, Carl had penetrated the wall around her heart.

What was she to do? She had never expected anything like this to happen. She was in love but unable to express it, wanting to hear words of love from a man she didn't even trust. It was crazy.

All the way home on the plane, she had been unusually silent. Carl questioned her about it, but when she lied that nothing was the matter, he buried his face in a stack of business papers and left her to her thoughts the rest of the way home.

Memories of their honeymoon night swirled in her mind. Try as she might, she couldn't dispel the picture of the two of them at the height of their ecstasy.

Was Carl remembering? she wondered. From the looks of his concentration on business, nothing could be further from his mind. Had it meant so little to him?

Sandy had learned quite a bit about Carl from Julia. But she discovered there were other sides to his character she couldn't fathom.

His Houston home was beautiful. As a real-estate developer, he had learned a great deal about designs. He had drawn up the basic plans for his home, which was situated along a stretch of lush acreage set aside for a future golf course.

The home seemed huge to Sandy. It contained over 13,000 square feet of floor space. She wondered how the two of them would ever find each other in the many rooms on both the first and second floors.

There was a special exercise room where Carl worked out daily. It contained a private sauna with fifteen varying temperature and humidity controls and a balance bar along one wall, plus an exercise bicycle and weights.

Next to it was a laundry chute to the washroom, and beyond that was a dumbwaiter to the kitchen below.

Down the hall was a music room with an expensive stereo setup and a bookcase lined with volumes about composers and the great musicians of the world. Next to that was a separate library room with floor-to-ceiling shelves stacked with books of all types.

Carl had a private office with his own bath, a special red, free-standing tub with gold fixtures.

Sandy giggled when she saw it. It seemed so out of character for Carl with his polished exterior and businesslike manner.

His office was lined down one side with large picture windows overlooking a balcony lush with beautiful potted and hanging plants. From there, Sandy could see across the house to the other side, where the lower floor exhibited a stained-glass window near the swimming pool. The design in the window was a mermaid swimming beneath the frothy waters of the sea.

It was an unusual home, warm and inviting, yet imposing. It was not the kind of house one found casually sold on the open market. It had character, obviously imbued by its designer. It was a one-of-a-kind house, built to rigid specifications for its owner.

The lower floor had the customary kitchen and a huge living room with a marble staircase that wound gracefully up to the second floor. Sandy could picture Scarlett O'Hara floating down that staircase in her floor-length hoop skirt in a scene from *Gone With the Wind*.

The massive den featured a large-screen TV and a long bar stocked with all the finest liquors.

The house was built in the shape of a U around an Olympic-sized swimming pool in the backyard.

Carl showed Sandy around, casually mentioning the four bedrooms on the second floor but pausing for a long time in the master bedroom on the ground floor.

"I had this designed for myself," Carl said. Was there an almost apologetic tone to his voice?

Sandy blushed as she looked into the room and saw herself reflected over and over again in a series of full-length mirrors. Carl shot her a mischievous glance. His blue eyes twinkled. His meaning was clear. He expected the two of them to share this room.

Sandy's cheeks turned pink.

"Is it too garish for you?" Carl asked.

"Not when the lights are out," Sandy mumbled.

"I understand," Carl said softly. He stared at her for a long minute, his eyes searching her face.

She swallowed hard.

"I'll have draperies installed to cover the mirrors if you want," he offered.

"Y-you'd do that for me?"

"Of course," Carl said, as if it would be the most natural thing in the world for him to put her feelings first. "I'll do whatever it takes to make you comfortable."

"Why?" she asked.

"Because you're my wife," he said. But he didn't say, "Because I love you."

A deep sadness filled Sandy. What had she done? Carl was such a decent man. Yet she had allowed him to marry her, to become shackled to a wife he didn't love and who could never express her love for him.

The inner turmoil she felt was devastating. She had escaped Roland, but was this any better? The hurt she was feeling was not physical, but it was just as painful.

Sandy moved her few belongings into her new home. She invited her mother over for dinner and pretended to be happy. Apparently she was convincing, because her mother seemed satisfied that Sandy had finally found contentment.

She entertained Julia and Brut and Carl's family and never let on about the despair in her heart. At work, she took the good-natured kidding of her fellow employees about marrying the boss. But underneath the bright façade lurked a broken spirit.

One day Sandy saw Roland walking away from the junior department just as she was approaching. Of course he must know about her marriage now. He had stopped bothering her completely. She felt a wave of gratitude to Carl for that!

If she were single, Roland would not hesitate to approach her. He would still be making her life miserable. At least the marriage was keeping Roland away, even though it was costing her dearly in heartache.

There was only one thing to do, and she was good at it. She had been doing it for years. She would bury her problems in her work.

The new lines Sandy had ordered for the September promotion were beginning to trickle in. She set up a brand new display for the junior sports department. She held meetings every morning to fill in her workers on the latest fashions they would be selling soon and conducted little scenarios in which they practiced selling to each other.

Sandy checked other departments of the store to see how well coordinated the entire store appeared to a shopper.

While she retained her buyer position, Carl asked her to take on a larger role in the entire operation of the business.

Gradually they settled into a comfortable relationship at work. Sandy knew what to expect on the job, how to react to Carl at the store, how often to intrude in his office and when to stay away.

But at home, the heartache came back. During their lovemaking, Carl was always passionate, considerate and patient. It was she who always lost control of her reserve with him in bed. But afterward, she relived the same remorse and sadness she remembered only too well. How long could they continue living as man and wife in a one-sided marriage? How long before frustrations at work and stress from his real estate and other holdings would push him to his emotional limits and force him to take his anger out on her?

Carl seemed more and more pressured. Their mealtime conversations consisted of employee problems, inventory shortages, attempts to improve customer relations and maintain the Van Helmut image in the community. Then Carl would get off on the real-estate business and his investments.

At least it kept their relationship impersonal. Sandy shied away from anything intimate, except in the bedroom.

There were times when Sandy caught Carl looking at her with a peculiar expression. His blue eyes would dwell on her face intently. He would become very quiet, as if considering something.

She felt sure he was regretting the marriage. It had been a bold offer, probably just an excuse to get her in bed. Carl was not used to women refusing his advances. Sandy had presented him a major challenge. Besides, she had threatened to quit her job, and Carl probably decided keeping her on at the store was worth a considerable sacrifice. It wasn't as if he had been involved with anyone else at the time, so he probably figured, Why not? After all, he had told her he didn't know whether he was capable of love. So what better marriage partner could he have than someone who was involved in the operation of the store? But apparently he had changed his mind and wished he hadn't become involved in her problems.

One day Carl called her into his office.

"I need help with this new promotion," he said.

Sandy looked at him, startled. It was the first time he had ever admitted he needed something from her.

"What kind of help?"

"Ideas. Sit down."

He motioned to a chair, which Sandy then occupied. It seemed strange to deal with Carl on a business level. Only the night before, he had made love to her. And now he was talking to her as if she were still Sandy Carver, employee. Maybe he could turn his feelings on and off like a faucet, but she couldn't. No matter what they were doing, she was constantly aware of his presence as her husband. And she was always on guard.

"You know we're having an elaborate display in the furniture department next month. I've been working on it for weeks."

"Yes."

"Most of the groundwork has been laid. But there's something missing. I can't put my finger on it." He began to pace. "We need a special touch, something romantic to capture the imagination of the buying public. Something universal they can all identify with. We've talked about a space theme, but that didn't work out. Someone else suggested a historical motif. That has possibilities. But I need some more input. You know what we're planning . . . live mannequins, a special backdrop to feature the main display, live plants, a string quartet to play from time to time . . . You've kept up with the situation so far."

"Yes, and I think it's going to be a great promotion. It should call a lot of attention to the store and sell a lot of merchandise. You're going to wake up the buying public."

"That's exactly what I want to do . . . wake them up. Now, if I could find something to illustrate that theme, something that would look terrific in a newspaper display ad."

"How about Sleeping Beauty?" Sandy suggested. "Prince Charming woke her up. She was lying on a bed. It would be a natural for the furniture department."

Carl smiled at her. "Hey, that's not bad!" he exclaimed. "Not bad at all. Let me give it some thought . . . check it out with a few other things I have to consider."

The next day Sandy found out her idea had been accepted. Carl asked her to supply some fashions from her department for the live mannequins who would stand in the tableau dressed as kitchen helpers who had fallen asleep when Sleeping Beauty had fallen under the witch's spell.

Julia was kept busy designing sketches for Sleeping Beauty's special dress, which the alterations department was going to fashion from one of their evening dresses.

The workroom of the store buzzed with activity. A special platform for the bed was constructed. The drapery department hung purple velvet curtains behind the ornate gold bedposts on which Sleeping Beauty would recline.

Carl spent his time approving sketches for newspaper ads, overseeing the remodeling in the furniture department, sending messages back and forth to the various departments for all the items that had to be coordinated and working late hours in the workroom with the construction crew.

Sandy found out it was true that Carl knew every aspect of the business. He also never felt he was above performing any task necessary to keep the store operating smoothly. She had witnessed him waiting on a lady purchasing a ten-dollar scarf and had seen him sweeping a neglected aisle after closing time.

In the midst of all the activity, Julia and Brut got married. Sandy was her matron of honor, Carl the best man.

At the dance afterward, Carl loosened up and smiled at her, his blue eyes twinkling. They marched around the floor at arm's length during a polka. But when the band played a slow waltz, Carl pulled her to him, his strong arms enveloping her and holding her close to him.

"Remind you of our wedding?" Carl asked softly in her ear. His warm breath sent a tingle racing through her.

"Yes," she said, hoping she didn't sound overly enthusiastic. Could his reminiscing mean their wedding meant more to him than just an empty ceremony of convenience?

"If you had to do it over again, would you still go through with it?" he asked, leading her through the crowd skillfully as they kept time to the music.

Sandy shivered. She hadn't been prepared for such a direct question. She desperately wanted to ask him the same thing, but she didn't dare. Her heart would shatter into a million tiny pieces if he said no.

"That's a strange question," she replied, struggling to keep her voice calm.

"Just wondering," Carl murmured. He fell silent as they finished the dance.

A few minutes later, they stood talking to another couple. Carl had apparently forgotten all about what he had asked her moments before. But she hadn't.

She couldn't concentrate on the conversation for wondering why Carl had brought up such a subject. Was he that concerned about her feelings? Did he perhaps care for her a little, after all? Or was he regretting the marriage and wondering if she felt the same? Was he hinting it was time to call the whole thing off?

She hoped she was nodding in the appropriate places in the conversation. Her mind was filled with so many unanswered questions that she hadn't the vaguest notion what was being discussed.

As they stood talking, Carl slipped his arm around her waist. Her heart pounded. Was he enjoying their closeness, or was the gesture just for looks? After all, they were still newlyweds. The natural thing for him to do was to appear involved with her. Dared she hope that he was enjoying himself with her? That he was growing to care for her?

Carl looked down at her. His blue eyes masked all his emotions. Try as she might, she was unable to penetrate into the inner person and read anything in his expression.

Yes, there was a smile on his lips. There was a twinkle in his eyes. But was it because of his feelings for her? Or was it due to the occasion and the champagne being passed around?

Carl kept her close the rest of the evening. They danced, but their conversation was about trivial matters pertaining to Brut and Julia's wedding.

A deep longing grew in Sandy, a longing for Carl

to take her in his arms and tell her that he loved her. It began as a small vacant feeling in the pit of her stomach and gradually grew larger and larger. Before the evening was over, it was an all-consuming desire. Her whole body ached to hear the words that would make her Carl's not only in name, but also in his heart. She wanted him to love her, to tell her that he loved her, and she wanted to whisper that she desperately loved him, too.

"You seem awfully quiet tonight," Carl said as he pulled the car into the garage.

"I'm just tired." She smiled weakly. She couldn't bear to look directly at him. She knew dark shadows would be playing across his face from the light in the garage. She knew her heart would swell with pain as she looked at his arresting features, which she had long ago memorized. It was hard enough seeing him in her mind's eye, so tall, handsome and masterful, so in charge of the world, so confident. But to look at Carl in person was more than her fragile emotions could bear.

He came around to her side of the car and opened the door for her. She slipped out. He stood close. She had to brush up next to him to get by. She felt his warmth and looked away.

"Sandy, you looked beautiful tonight," he said.

Her breath caught in her throat. Involuntarily her eyes darted to his face. His smile was soft, inviting. Little lines ran from the corners of his eyes and disappeared. His head was tilted toward hers.

She froze to the spot, longing to tear her gaze away from his but unable to.

Gently he tilted her chin up with one hand.

Her muscles tensed.

226

Slowly Carl leaned toward her, his lips brushing hers lightly. Sparks of fire ignited in her.

Her mouth tingled where their lips had met.

Carl pulled back, looked at her with his blue eyes narrowed in a thoughtful expression, and then slipped his hand in hers.

She could hardly breathe. But she forced a smile.

Carl continued looking at her in a strange way while they entered the house.

"Coffee?" he asked as they passed by the kitchen.

"No, thank you," she said. It was a struggle to keep her voice sounding calm. She didn't understand what was happening, but she felt some sort of tension building. She knew he was leading her to bed, but it was more than that. There was an electricity in the air she had never felt before. What it was she couldn't define, but she definitely felt it.

In their bedroom, they undressed silently. When Sandy went into the bathroom, Carl said, "I'll be waiting for you."

She wanted to answer, "Yes, my love." But she didn't dare. Probably Carl was only responding to the mood of the wedding, reliving the excitement and anticipation of their first night together. Brut's marriage had struck some chord in Carl. She knew it was nothing personal as far as she was concerned.

Her husband was in an amorous mood, not because he really loved her but because he was caught up in the events of the evening.

Sadly Sandy undressed and slipped into a long gold nightgown with sequined straps and an empire waistline. It was the sort of gown a woman should wear to go to bed with her husband. He would gently slip the straps off her shoulders and run his hand down her back. Then he would bite her on the neck, sending waves of desire coursing through her. Soon the gown would be lying on the floor, a silent testimony to their lovemaking. The room would be silent except for an occasional moan of pleasure. But her heart would not be silent. It would be calling out to Carl, asking him to love her. But he would never hear its plea.

Sandy wiped a tear from her eyes. She sniffed and dabbed a spot of powder on her cheeks and blended it to cover the redness of her eyelids.

She hoped Carl wouldn't notice she had been crying. But then why should he? She was very clever at covering up her true feelings. She was madly in love with him, but he had never noticed that either, had never read it in her eyes or in the expression on her face. Maybe he hadn't noticed because he didn't want to.

Sandy joined Carl. He smiled at her before turning the lights down low. They became two shadowy figures casting their reflections on the far wall, two figures enjoying the fruits of the other's body but never expressing any real love.

After that night, Sandy felt more strained with Carl than before. To keep herself from brooding about her problems, Sandy took on all the tasks she could find at work. She volunteered to work in the alterations room, to help Julia with her copy for the newspaper campaign, to run errands between departments, to sell on the floor in the junior department. She was eager to do anything that would keep her mind and her hands busy and out of Carl's way.

She rarely saw him during those weeks except when she passed him in the store and when they went to bed. She ate most of her meals in the coffee shop or the delicatessen across the street.

Carl was so busy himself that he didn't seem to notice. At sales meetings, he treated her like any other employee.

Julia had agreed to finish out the month and would be leaving then to be simply Mrs. Brut Van Helmut. Sandy met the replacement Julia was training and laughed hollowly when the new employee asked what her chances were for marrying one of the Van Helmuts.

Cautiously Sandy looked for any more signs of Roland. But he seemed to have dropped out of her life. It was too soon for her to believe he really would no longer bother her. He was not one to give up easily. But at least there was no sign of him hanging around anymore. For that, she was grateful.

It was a week before Van Helmut's unveiling of the new fall display in the furniture department. The store was in an absolute frenzy.

Carl had ordered a spinning wheel from a manufacturer of odd items, but it was long past due. The purple velvet bedspread for Sleeping Beauty's bed had failed to arrive, and a lamp with a Sleeping Beauty motif had been broken in transit.

Carl found Sandy discussing a display with Deanna. He called her aside.

"Stop whatever you're doing. I'm going to put you on the trail of these missing items right now. Do whatever you have to to get them here on time. We'll fly them in if necessary. We can't have this promotion ruined at the last minute."

"Can't we make substitutions?" Sandy asked.

"We could find another bedspread, perhaps, and we could even do without the lamp. But there's no

229

place else to go for the spinning wheel but Danche's in Minnesota. Do what you can about the other items, but get me that spinning wheel!"

"All right," Sandy said. "Consider it taken care of."

"I knew I could count on you," Carl said.

A little feather of pride tickled her, and she smiled.

Carl started to hurry off, but he stopped momentarily for a double take.

"You ought to smile more often," he said.

What did he mean by that, she thought hotly. Was he accusing her of being a sourpuss?

But he was gone before she could ask him.

Sandy hurried to the spare desk in the main office and carted over a directory of manufacturers. She located Danche's and dialed the number. A telephone answering machine spouted out a recorded message. She left her name and number but doubted he would return her call. She remembered they had ordered something from the same place a couple of years before; it was a small outfit run by a cantankerous old man who didn't seem to care whether he sold anything or not.

Sandy scribbled out a telegram to Danche's, briefly explaining the problem and asking for a phone call. She also said she'd try to call again the following day just before lunch. She phoned in the telegram and then dictated a letter to one of the secretaries. That she would send by Federal Express. It would arrive the next morning.

She would bombard Danche's with demands for the spinning wheel. She'd get through to the little old man somehow. He'd reply just to get her to leave him alone, if for no other reason.

Next, Sandy called the shipper for the lamp and explained the problem. He promised to send out another one on the next bus.

When she contacted the supplier for the bedspread, she was told she would have to wait until the next day for information. The girl on the phone said their computers were down and would be inoperable until then.

Carl no longer seemed interested in Sandy sexually. All their conversations revolved around the promotion. He came home late at night, tired and ready for bed. He was out of the store much of the time settling details that involved the branch stores.

Sandy finally got a billing number on the bedspread and traced it. It arrived the middle of the week. The lamp came in undamaged this time. But the spinning wheel was still a problem.

"I've done everything I know how," Sandy said dismally to Carl on Thursday. "We're all set for the promotion to be unveiled Saturday, and Sleeping Beauty is going to be minus her spinning wheel. We've featured a wheel in all our ads. Do you suppose we can just quietly ignore the fact that we don't have one in the display?"

"We could," Carl said. "But we won't. That's not the way I do things. You should know that by now, Sandy. At Van Helmut's it's first class all the way. We've featured a spinning wheel in our promotions, and we're going to have one here in the store. I'll take care of it."

A wave of disappointment spread over Sandy. She didn't know why it mattered, but it bothered her that she had let Carl down.

"No," she said. "That's my job. I haven't given up yet."

Carl smiled at her. "Good girl," he said. She noted the approval in his voice, and it warmed a forgotten spot of her heart. That it affected her at all surprised her.

Sandy got on the phone and called Danche's every thirty minutes. She left messages on the recorder. Finally, she got hold of a live person.

"Oh, I'm sure that has been shipped," said a female voice on the other end of the line.

"What's the bill number?" Sandy asked.

"Well, I don't know," the voice said.

"If it's been shipped, there will be a bill number," Sandy said. "Will you look it up for me please? I can track it down if I have that number."

"Would you like for me to call you back on that?" the girl asked.

"No, I'll hold on," Sandy said.

"Just a moment." The line clicked, and Sandy thought for a moment she had been cut off. Frustration boiled in her.

But a few moments later a man's voice spoke to her.

"Van Helmut's?" came the shaky voice.

"Yes," Sandy said. "We ordered a spinning wheel for a special promotion. It should have been here by now. I'm trying to get the bill number. I want the name of the shipper. Are you Mr. Danche?"

"Yes."

"Mr. Danche, this is very important to us. Please, give me the information I need."

There was a pause. "Here it is," Mr. Danche said. "It was shipped last Wednesday. Should have been there by now." He gave her the number she needed and the name of the shipper.

Another phone call to the shipper led her to a trucking line that connected with another trucking line, which delivered in Houston. At last she was getting closer to her prey.

The second trucking line said they knew nothing about the shipment. But Sandy refused to accept that. She insisted on talking to the manager, who thumbed through some papers and gave her the same story.

"All right, you don't have the paper work," she said. "But perhaps you have the shipment. Will you send someone to check the loading dock? This is very important. I'll hang on."

There was a disgusted sigh at the other end, but Sandy heard the phone being laid down and breathed easier.

It was some time before the man returned to the phone and said the package had been found. However, there was no way it could reach Van Helmut's the following day by truck.

"Will you put it on the bus for me?" Sandy asked. "I'll pay you your regular shipping charges, plus a bonus for your trouble. If you get it on the bus tonight, it will be here tomorrow. Will you do that?"

There was a pause.

"Okay," said the voice.

Sandy made the necessary arrangements by phone for the bus she needed and called the information back to the trucking line.

She would be a tangled knot of nerves until the following night. Only then would she know if the truck dispatcher had actually complied with her request. If he hadn't, there would be no way to get the spinning wheel delivered on time.

She had done all she could, she told herself.

"I hope it makes it," Sandy said to Carl when she told him everything she had done.

"I do, too," he said. "The TV stations are sending out a crew for a short segment on the news. Seems our Sleeping Beauty display has become the current rage around town. Everyone is talking about it. In addition to our ad, the newspaper is going to feature the display on the front page of the business section in Sunday's paper."

"Great!" Sandy exclaimed. "It should be very good for business."

"That's the whole idea," Carl said, smiling. The skin around his eyes crinkled.

Sandy couldn't help looking at him in a way that disturbed her. Why couldn't she relax around him and be herself? She wasn't sure what "herself" was anymore. She had kept the real Sandy so tightly wrapped, like a mummy, that she wasn't sure if she'd recognize the real her anymore.

The next day was another frenzy of activity, including last-minute details that always arose no matter how carefully mapped out they were.

Sandy planned to meet the 6:00 P.M. bus carrying the spinning wheel. Carl agreed to let her go because it would still be light. He refused to allow her to drive into that part of town alone at night.

Carl was working late at the store. Sandy was to pick up the package, take it directly to the store and then go home. Sandy was both furious and dismayed when the bus yielded no package. There was another one in an hour. Perhaps the man had missed the designated bus. She'd wait.

The next bus was another disappointment. Sandy got on the phone and tried to call the trucking line.

Someone answered the phone. In the background she heard the muffled sounds of trucks being loaded. She persuaded the dispatcher to look for her package. He was the night man, not the one she had spoken to earlier, so he knew nothing about it. He could not find it anywhere and said the paper work indicated it had arrived but had not been put on any of their trucks.

Sandy became frantic. There was another bus in an hour. Should she wait, hoping the package was on that one, or was she just wasting her time? Carl wouldn't like it if she stayed in this part of town after dark. It was a rough, mean neighborhood. At night, it was called the Cut because of the many stabbings that occurred regularly.

Sandy looked around her at the seedy types who filtered in and out of the place. Out the window, the sky had turned black. She paced the concrete floor, uncertain of what to do.

Finally, she decided to wait for one more bus. If the package was not on that one, she would reluctantly give up.

When the next bus pulled in, Sandy stood as close to the package-receiving office as she could. She eyed each parcel as it was hauled through the door. There was no way she could read all the labels on the boxes on the bottom of the stack, so she edged up to the window.

"Well?" she asked the clerk, who had made two futile searches already.

He smiled and nodded. "It's here," he said, lifting a large cardboard crate onto the ledge next to him.

Sandy sighed. Relief washed over her. At last!

"Do you want someone to load it into your car?" he asked.

"Please, yes," Sandy said. Eyeing the box, she thought she could carry it, but she didn't like the idea of traipsing out onto the sidewalk alone at this time of night in this neighborhood.

An attendant shoved the box in the front seat next to her, and Sandy took off with a feeling of jubilation.

All the many preparations for this special promotion had been a nightmare. There had been weeks of planning, hundreds of details to work out, countless phone calls, meetings and conferences. The paper work piled up; there had been hurt feelings and angry employees and unexpected complications.

But gradually all the problems had been worked out except for the spinning wheel. Now it had arrived, and Sandy would drop it off at the store on her way home. The last-minute assembling could be done before it was added to the display in preparation for the opening.

A familiar sense of accomplishment spread over Sandy. It was the first time she had felt like her old self since Roland had come back into her life. She had taken on a major challenge and had succeeded. It reminded her of the style show, of the promotion she had sought and won when she moved up from the candy counter, of the time she advanced to buyer of her department.

She enjoyed battling adversity and coming out on top. It gave her a sense of control over her destiny; it made her feel good about herself.

So why was she unable to cope with the adversity in her marriage to Carl? Why couldn't she forget the past and enjoy herself in his arms? Even though he didn't love her, she loved him, and it was a tragedy that she had to waste those moments when he held her close and shared with her the most intimate moments two people can spend together.

Was it because she had learned to conquer external obstacles only and not internal ones?

Sandy arrived at the store and parked her car in the lot. She hauled the box from the front seat and hurried to the back entrance.

It was locked. Carl obviously thought the package had not arrived and had locked the door, thinking she had gone on home from the bus station.

Sandy put the box down. After their marriage, Carl had given her a set of keys to all the doors at the store. She let herself in and dragged the box in behind her. It was getting heavy.

She closed the door behind her.

She left the box sitting there and went to look for Carl. The interior lights burned softly. There was something spooky about the empty store at night. Her footsteps echoed over the terrazzo floors of the aisles with a hollow, melancholy sound.

"Carl?" Sandy called. The only sound was the low hum of the air conditioning.

Maybe Carl was in the furniture department taking care of last-minute details for the display. Sandy looked around her. It was creepy to be in the store all alone. She hurried to the escalator. It was not running at such a late hour. She walked up it.

Her eyes darted right and left. Carl was nowhere to be seen. Sandy felt suddenly very alone and a little afraid. To calm herself, she directed her attention to the Sleeping Beauty display. It was magnificent.

To the left was a kitchen display with an old iron oven and a large wooden chopping block. Live mannequins would dress in old-fashioned clothes and drape themselves around the scene to represent the sleeping household. On a higher platform sat a beautiful gold bedstead. The royal-purple velvet bedspread was trimmed with gold cording; a matching drapery hung on the wall behind it. Live doves were caged outside a window backdrop, through which a live tree could be seen.

Each day, models would take shifts as Sleeping Beauty and Prince Charming in a tableau of their final moments before he kissed her.

The spinning wheel would go to the left of the bed.

It was a beautiful scene, but Sandy felt a chill race along her spinal cord. She hadn't known the store could feel so scary. She was eager to find Carl.

He was probably in the workroom. Suddenly, every light in the store went off. She was plunged into inky darkness.

Sandy stood immobile, not understanding what the unexpected darkness meant.

She froze. She couldn't see a thing, but she heard muffled sounds emanating from somewhere around her.

Don't panic! she told herself. It must be a power failure. No one but Carl and a couple of workers could be in the store. She had come in the back way and had locked the door behind her . . . hadn't she?

Or had she merely closed it?

She couldn't remember.

Was it possible Carl had already gone home? He might have finished his work and left, assuming the spinning wheel had not arrived and she had gone home from the bus station.

Was she in the store all alone?

If she was, what were those sounds she heard? Was it someone walking around in the store somewhere?

Was it someone looking for her?

Was it someone who had come in the back door?

Should she call out for Carl?

Chapter Twelve

Sandy's mouth felt dry, her knees weak.

It was dark. She couldn't see a thing. She turned. Which way had she come?

She took a tentative step forward, her hands feeling ahead of her in the darkness. She took another step. Her hand hit something.

She gasped. She jerked her hands back, covering her mouth with them.

She retreated. She heard a sound nearby. Her heart pounded frantically. Her lips trembled.

She strained to see in the darkness. But it was too black to make out anything.

She stepped back. Something brushed across her face.

Sandy flinched. She couldn't catch her breath. A smothering sensation threatened her.

Panic overwhelmed her. She had to find the exit!

She turned and ran. She bumped into an object. Her hand shot out to protect her. It touched a heavy fabric. When her fingers clutched it, she heard a scraping noise and something heavy fell against her.

She screamed. Something fell over her and covered her entire body. She flailed her arms around wildly, trying to shove it away from her.

Ragged moans tore from her throat. She fell, scrambled to her feet, throwing off the covering, and ran blindly.

She thudded against something. A sharp pain shot up her leg. She was dimly aware of a warmth oozing down her ankle.

There was a loud crash, the shattering explosion of ceramic or glass breaking, and then a deathly silence.

Suddenly, the lights blazed on. Sandy blinked, frantically looking around her. It was a moment before she saw what had happened.

She was too concerned about her own safety and her fear of being attacked to realize what she had done.

Only after she reassured herself that no one was pursuing her—that she was alone—did the scene around her register on her senses. A sob of anguish escaped her lips as she eyed the wreckage around her.

She stood in the middle of the Sleeping Beauty display. The special lamp lay shattered on the floor. The royal purple drapery had been ripped from its rod. Two small tables had been overturned, one of them damaged.

The place was a shambles. She was horrified at what she had done. Her head throbbed so hard that she wasn't aware of the pain in her leg, where blood spurted from a deep wound.

Then she heard footsteps on the motionless escalator. There was someone in the store! And all her clamoring to get away from him had signaled where she was.

Her gaze was riveted on the top of the escalator. The footsteps grew louder. Her breathing stopped.

A thatch of blond hair emerged over the top of the railing. Sandy cried out. Her scream turned to a sob as she recognized Carl's face.

A shudder of relief ran through her. She wanted to run into his arms and cry out her fear. But she stood rooted to the spot.

Carl's blue eyes darted around the room. His face turned pale. He scowled.

Sandy glanced around her once again. Torn draperies, a shattered lamp and broken furniture surrounded her. She had destroyed the Sleeping Beauty display!

She longed to run to Carl and beg his forgiveness, to tell him how ashamed and sorry she was for her foolishness that had resulted in this mess. But she couldn't move.

The imposing frame of Carl began to advance toward her. His eyes blazed darkly.

Suddenly, it was not Carl she saw bearing down on her. It was the image of Roland superimposed over Carl. She was no longer standing amid the wreckage of the Sleeping Beauty display. Her time frame shifted. She dissolved into the past. She was cowering in the midst of the shambles of the paintings Roland had worked so hard to produce. Paintings that she had damaged.

It was not Carl striding toward her. It was Roland

towering over her, about to strike her, to beat and kick her. Roland . . . insane with rage.

Then Roland's face faded and it was Carl.

A paralyzing fear gripped her. It was a replay of all her terror and humiliation, of her unrelenting sadness and wrath over her disastrous first marriage. She stood immobile, unable to flee or fight, knowing only what was sure to come. She could not speak or blink her eyes. She was transfixed with an agonizing anticipation that the figure lumbering toward her was about to unleash upon her the pain she recalled only too well.

She whimpered, "Please—please don't . . ." She raised her arms to ward off the first blows.

She squeezed her eyes shut and waited. But instead of the blinding pain of attack, she felt strong arms slip around her, lifting her off the floor, gently cradling her head in the crook of an elbow.

"Sandy, Sandy," Carl murmured. His voice throbbed with concern.

Sandy opened her eyes. Did she see tears in Carl's eyes?

"You're hurt," he said tenderly.

He supported her with his knees and reached down for the torn purple-velvet drapery. With a strong pull, he tore off a section and folded it into a pad. He placed it against her throbbing leg and placed her hand on it to hold it. Then he ripped another piece to tie around her leg, to hold the elegant bandage in place.

"That ought to stop the blood."

Gently he lifted her and stepped up onto the platform. He placed her on the bed in the center of the display.

Carl's eyes searched her face as he touched her

lightly on the chin, turning her head from side to side. "Are you all right?" he asked. "What happened?"

"The lights went off. I—I couldn't find you and thought maybe you'd already left. I heard noises. I was scared. I thought somebody was after me. I panicked."

"Oh, Sandy, I'm so sorry. When you didn't return, I figured the spinning wheel hadn't arrived. I thought you'd gone home. I was working late. You must have heard the last of the workmen leaving just before I switched some of the light connections from the workroom. I was checking the extra lights for the display when I heard all the commotion. You're still shaking." His voice was soothing, concerned.

He took her in his arms and held her close. For the first time, she melted against him, totally comfortable in his arms. He had every right to be furious at her. Instead, he was so worried about her he hadn't even mentioned the display!

Carl pulled back a moment and took a long look at her. She returned his gaze squarely. A smile crossed his lips. He moved closer to her, his mouth finding hers and locking her in a masterful kiss. Then he rained kisses all over her face, caressing her, holding her gently to him and arranging the pillows on the bed to make her more comfortable.

"How's your leg?" he asked.

"I—I don't know. It hurts."

"I'll check it." He slowly lifted the makeshift bandage. She winced.

"The bleeding's stopped," he said, smiling.

"Good."

His large, luminous eyes trailed up to her face.

She sensed he saw only her, nothing else, not the damage she had created, not the department they were in, not the dress she wore, nothing except her.

She was drawn to him by the expression on his face, by the obvious lack of concern for anything but her and her well-being. Needles of guilt and remorse pricked her.

"I—I made such a mess," she said. She wanted to apologize, but it seemed futile. Nothing she said could repair the damage to the display.

"Oh, Carl, I'm so sorry. Aren't you furious at me?"

"Furious? Of course not," Carl said gently. "We can fix it. The main thing is you, that you're all right. When I first saw you standing there, I couldn't figure out what had happened. But I knew you were afraid. The look on your face, the terror in your eyes . . . then that gash on your leg."

"All caused by my stupidity!"

"It wasn't stupid," Carl said. "Anyone would have been afraid under the circumstances . . . alone in a blackened department store at night. You reacted normally, Sandy."

She looked at him. The last vestiges of animosity toward him flickered away. For the first time since her marriage to Carl, she began to trust him, to understand the person he really was.

The trust began as a glimmer like a tiny light in a tunnel and grew until it suffused her entire being with light and warmth. His kindness and concern, in spite of the damage she'd done, overwhelmed her. He had every right to be furious with her. But he showed only tenderness.

He was no longer a stranger, cold and remote at

times. Carl Van Helmut was a good man, kind and considerate and loving. It was as simple as that!

Why hadn't she been able to see his true being? Why had he seemed such an enigma? Was it her own distrust and fear of men that had built the wall between them and made him seem so distant?

Something like a cold, hard knot that had kept her true feelings locked away for so many years suddenly began to melt away.

Sandy leaned her head against him, feeling truly safe and secure in his arms for the first time. A tear slid from under her eyelids and down her cheeks.

Tentatively, she wrapped her arms around his neck and looked him full in the face.

Carl smiled. "Sandy—Sandy, I love you," he whispered.

Tears ran down her cheeks. "You—you *what?*"

"Yes, I do love you," he exclaimed, holding her in a tender embrace. "I wasn't sure of my feelings when I asked you to marry me, but there's no longer any doubt in my mind. I love you with all my heart and being as I've never loved anyone else in my life. I love you more than life itself. You have become my life."

His mouth found hers. She was sobbing and kissing him at the same time. Her heart felt as if it couldn't contain all the joy she felt without bursting.

Carl ran his warm hands down her back, his skin caressing her flesh. She molded herself to him, desperately wanting to be his in every way, eager to be held and kissed and roused to a fever pitch of ecstasy.

She felt her dress slip off her shoulders. Cool air conditioning whisked across her bare flesh. She shivered, but not from the cold. It was a shiver of delight, a sense of freedom and abandonment from old restraints.

She couldn't believe this was happening!

Carl took her hand and put it to his shirt. Her fingers willingly unbuttoned it and slid inside to find the mat of curly, thick hair on his chest.

Carl pulled her to him, almost crushing her in his arms. Strong, hard muscles encircled her back. She felt safe and secure in his arms. She snuggled to him, nuzzling her head in his neck, nibbling the skin along his muscular shoulders.

Carl slid off her bra. Goose bumps popped out all along her arm. He moved her hands to his belt line. She gave him a questioning look.

He nodded.

For a moment, she didn't understand.

Then a smile crept onto her lips. She returned his nod and slowly pulled his shirt from his trousers.

Of course she wanted him to go on! Never mind that they were in the middle of the furniture department of Van Helmut's department store. The place was deserted except for them.

Carl finished removing his shirt and lay down beside Sandy on the Sleeping Beauty bed. His hands caressed her slowly, and she rode one crescendo after another on the way to heights of rapture.

Passion so long smothered in her broke free with a violent storm. Gone forever were the misgivings and uncertainty about her marriage. Carl was her man. She was his woman. They had been destined to meet, to love, to belong together for all eternity.

The past was all behind her now. She was another woman in another era with another man. He had broken down the old barriers to the smoldering desire underneath the iceberg she had created around herself. In its place was a steaming volcano, ready to spew forth its hot, molten lava in a dazzling display of its new-found energy.

Beside the bed lay the clothes of a man and a woman swept away on a tide of emotional intensity. The store was completely silent except for the murmurings of two lovers entwined in each other's arms, giving themselves to one another in a heady well-spring of exotic bliss.

In the middle of the damaged display, like the phoenix rising from its ashes, the new, vigorous and completely restored response of Sandy Van Helmut sprang forth. She melted in Carl's arms; she moaned with pleasure and longing; she gave as much as she took.

And she enjoyed every second of it.

Carl drove her to new heights of ecstasy, way beyond her wildest imaginings.

At last she was free. Free to love, free to be herself, free to enjoy, free to take all life had to offer, free to give herself, body, soul and heart, to a man again. Most of all, she was free to trust life, to trust her own feelings.

She trusted Carl with everything she had inside her. She made up for all the lost years, and the release, when it came, was dramatic and complete.

She fell limp in Carl's arms. She was perspiring, breathing hard and smiling.

Carl grinned at her. "When you let loose, you're really something!"

She sighed. "When you came in and discovered the damage I'd caused—time turned back for me. For a moment, it was that horrible scene when I'd fallen into Roland's paintings and destroyed them. I was terrified. I—I thought you were going to beat me. But you were so tender and gentle, concerned only about me. Suddenly, I realized all men are not like Roland. You are not Roland, you're Carl. I don't ever have to be a captive of the past again!"

"Sandy," he murmured. "I'm so glad! Tonight was beautiful and perfect. And that's how our love life is going to be from now on."

Carl lifted himself up on one elbow. He curled a tendril of her long blond hair around one finger. "Sandy, I love you," he said. "I'm never going to let you go."

She bit her lower lip. Her heart throbbed from joy. He loved her! She said the words over and over to herself.

"At first, I wasn't sure how I felt about you," he went on. "I can't say for sure why I offered to marry you. Maybe I loved you and didn't want to admit it to myself. I had always prided myself on making it on my own. It was hard for me to admit I needed anybody else. But I couldn't let you get away from me. If it hadn't worked out . . . if you had left me, I would never have married again. You're the only woman in my life, Sandy, and the only woman I could ever love. Say you'll stay with me."

"Oh, Carl," she choked. "If you only knew how much I love you. But I couldn't tell you. I was so mixed up inside. It took you to teach me to trust again, to be able to love again."

Carl smiled and pulled her to him, wrapping his arms around her protectively.

"Do you want a wife who's going to be afraid every time she steps out of the house that her ex-husband may be lurking around? That's why I ruined the display. When the lights went out, I couldn't remember if I had locked the service door behind me. I thought maybe Roland was following me and had trapped me here in the store. He's still hanging around, Carl."

"Not anymore," Carl said. "I caught him sneaking around the junior department last week. I didn't know who he was at first, but one of the girls in your department said he'd been there some time before asking about you. It was obvious who he was. I told him to leave. When I told him who I was, he realized he couldn't fight the entire Van Helmut family. By now, he's long gone, fled to another state. He won't ever bother you again, Sandy."

Carl squeezed her tightly, and she melted against him. They lay together on the bed for a while, just enjoying being in each other's arms.

Then Carl kissed her again. He looked at her, a question on his face. She knew what he was asking.

Carl's hand trailed down her shoulder and toward the soft flesh that stirred in her a quickening of the pulse. She had a lot of lost time to make up for, and she wasn't about to waste another minute of it. She nodded.

"Yes, Prince Charming, your Sleeping Beauty has awakened. . . ."

MORE ROMANCE FOR
A SPECIAL WAY TO RELAX
$1.95 each

2 ☐ Hastings	21 ☐ Hastings	41 ☐ Halston	60 ☐ Thorne
3 ☐ Dixon	22 ☐ Howard	42 ☐ Drummond	61 ☐ Beckman
4 ☐ Vitek	23 ☐ Charles	43 ☐ Shaw	62 ☐ Bright
5 ☐ Converse	24 ☐ Dixon	44 ☐ Eden	63 ☐ Wallace
6 ☐ Douglass	25 ☐ Hardy	45 ☐ Charles	64 ☐ Converse
7 ☐ Stanford	26 ☐ Scott	46 ☐ Howard	65 ☐ Cates
8 ☐ Halston	27 ☐ Wisdom	47 ☐ Stephens	66 ☐ Mikels
9 ☐ Baxter	28 ☐ Ripy	48 ☐ Ferrell	67 ☐ Shaw
10 ☐ Thiels	29 ☐ Bergen	49 ☐ Hastings	68 ☐ Sinclair
11 ☐ Thornton	30 ☐ Stephens	50 ☐ Browning	69 ☐ Dalton
12 ☐ Sinclair	31 ☐ Baxter	51 ☐ Trent	70 ☐ Clare
13 ☐ Beckman	32 ☐ Douglass	52 ☐ Sinclair	71 ☐ Skillern
14 ☐ Keene	33 ☐ Palmer	53 ☐ Thomas	72 ☐ Belmont
15 ☐ James	35 ☐ James	54 ☐ Hohl	73 ☐ Taylor
16 ☐ Carr	36 ☐ Dailey	55 ☐ Stanford	74 ☐ Wisdom
17 ☐ John	37 ☐ Stanford	56 ☐ Wallace	75 ☐ John
18 ☐ Hamilton	38 ☐ John	57 ☐ Thornton	76 ☐ Ripy
19 ☐ Shaw	39 ☐ Milan	58 ☐ Douglass	77 ☐ Bergen
20 ☐ Musgrave	40 ☐ Converse	59 ☐ Roberts	78 ☐ Gladstone

MORE ROMANCE FOR
A SPECIAL WAY TO RELAX

$2.25 each

79 ☐ Hastings	82 ☐ McKenna	85 ☐ Beckman	88 ☐ Saxon
80 ☐ Douglass	83 ☐ Major	86 ☐ Halston	89 ☐ Meriwether
81 ☐ Thornton	84 ☐ Stephens	87 ☐ Dixon	90 ☐ Justin

LOOK FOR WAY OF THE WILLOW
BY LINDA SHAW

Silhouette Intimate Moments

Coming Soon

Dreams Of Evening by Kristin James

Tonio Cruz was a part of Erica Logan's past and she hated him for betraying her. Then he walked back into her life and Erica's fear of loving him again was nothing compared to her fear that he would discover the one secret link that still bound them together.

Once More With Feeling by Nora Roberts

Raven and Brand—charismatic, temperamental, talented. Their songs had once electrified the world. Now, after a separation of five years, they were to be reunited to create their special music again. The old magic was still there, but would it be enough to mend two broken hearts?

Emeralds In The Dark by Beverly Bird

Courtney Winston's sight was fading, but she didn't need her eyes to know that Joshua Knight was well worth loving. If only her stubborn pride would let her compromise, but she refused to tie any man to her when she knew that someday he would have to be her eyes.

Sweetheart Contract by Pat Wallace

Wynn Carson, trucking company executive, and Duke Bellini, union president, were on opposite sides of the bargaining table. But once they got together in private, they were very much on the same side.

Coming Next Month

Love's Gentle Chains by Sondra Stanford

Lynn had fled from Drew believing she didn't belong in his
world. Then she discovered she was bound to him by her love
and the child he had unknowingly fathered.

All's Fair by Lucy Hamilton

Automotive engineer Kitty Gordon had been in love with race
driver Steve Duncan when she was sixteen. But this time, she
would find the inside track to his heart.

Love Feud by Anne Lacey

Carole returned to the hills of North Carolina
and rediscovered Jon. His family was still an anathema to
hers, but he drew her to him with a sensuous spell she
was unable to resist.

Cry Mercy, Cry Love by Monica Barrie

Heather Strand, although blind since birth, saw more clearly
than Reid Hunter until love sharpened his vision and he
realized that Heather was the only woman for him—forever.

A Matter Of Trust by Emily Doyle

After being used by one man, Victoria Van Straaten wanted
to keep Andreas at arm's length. However, on a cruise to
Crete she found Andreas determined to close the distance.

Dreams Lost, Dreams Found by Pamela Wallace

It was as though Brynne was reliving a Scottish legend with
Ross Fleming—descendant of the Lord of the Isles. Only this
time the legend would have a happy ending.